Mistress
of Luke's Folly

Mistress of Luke's Folly

ELIZABETH ELGIN

G.K. Hall & Co. • **Chivers Press**
Thorndike, Maine USA   Bath, England

This Large Print edition is published by G.K. Hall & Co., USA
and by Chivers Press, England.

Published in 1997 in the U.S. by arrangement with
Caroline Sheldon Literary Agency.

Published in 1997 in the U.K. by arrangement with
HarperCollins Publishers Ltd.

U.S.   Softcover   0-7838-8261-0   (Paperback Collection Edition)
U.K.   Hardcover   0-7540-3094-6   (Chivers Large Print)

The text of this Large Print edition is unabridged.
Other aspects of the book may vary from the original edition.

Set in 16 pt. Plantin by Al Chase.

Printed in the United States on permanent paper.

British Library Cataloging in Publication Data available

Library of Congress Cataloging in Publication Data

Elgin, Elizabeth.
    Mistress of Luke's Folly / Elizabeth Elgin.
       p.   cm.
    ISBN 0-7838-8261-0   (lg. print : sc : alk. paper)
    I. Title.
    [PR6055.L37M57   1997]
    823'.914—dc21   97-24397

Mistress
of Luke's Folly

One

"Just wait until I tell them!"

Instantly it seemed as if the sun was shining and every bird in creation singing fit to burst its little throat. Sarah Makin was going to be a lady-clerk! She was on her way up in the world and, by Old Lud, she'd show them!

But who would have thought it? Who could possibly have imagined such a thing could happen? She had awakened to the same grey morning, she reasoned breathlessly, to the same hopelessness that each day brought. There had been the same insistent rattling on the window pane from Ned's five o'clock pole. So how could she possibly have known something so wonderful was just around the corner?

There were no alarm-clocks in Canal Street. The mill-workers of the Three-streets put their trust instead in Limping Ned. Six days a week Ned rattled his pole against the windows of Canal Street, Albert Court and Tinker's Row, shattering dreams, calling young and old to face another day, a day as drab as yesterday that was gone and tomorrow, still to come.

Sarah had opened her eyes then quickly closed them. Why couldn't today be Sunday so she might sleep on, lie quiet in her bed until the ache was soothed from her bones and the mill noise

7

that beat inside her head was silenced?

Folk here in Hollinsdyke swore God Himself was a mill-owner but Sarah knew for sure He wasn't. If God had owned Low Clough mill there'd have been no day of rest.

The rattling came again.

"Coming!" She threw back the blanket, pattering barefoot to draw aside the blind.

In the street below Ned waited patiently for a sign that she was awake. He was a good knocker-up; always waited until he was sure, and all for tuppence a week.

Sarah raised her hand and the little man nodded, then dragging his withered foot across the gas-lit cobbles, limped on to the next soot-blackened window.

"One day," Sarah whispered, "I'll get back into bed and Luke Holroyd and his looms can go to the devil!"

But not this morning, for today was reckoning-day at the mill, the day that made sense of the rest of the week. Tomorrow she would be penniless again, but tonight, for just a little while, there would be ten silver shillings shining bright in her pocket.

From across the landing she heard the creak of her father's bed. Like Ned, her father was lame, but Ned had been born that way and Caleb Makin had not. Caleb's wasted leg and twisted shoulder were not the whim of the Almighty but the bitter outcome of a mill-master's meanness. True, Luke Holroyd's unguarded machines were breaking the law, but the knowledge sat easily on his conscience. Luke Holroyd was also a magistrate; he *was* the law in Hollinsdyke, so if his workers didn't watch what they were about it was their own fault. If a man tangled with a great iron cog or a child's hand was slashed by a powerstrap, it was nowt to do with him!

It was sad, Sarah sighed, to see her father so. Since the accident, he would often sit unspeaking, staring into the past, remembering when his body was whole and his wife alive. But those days were long gone, she reasoned. Now she was the breadwinner and Luke Holroyd owned her soul for twelve hours a day, six days a week.

She poured water into a bowl and splashed herself awake. She never ceased to marvel about the other world, that faraway place where people had rooms especially to wash in. She knew it was true. Her mother had told her about such things. There had been three bathrooms at Ainderby Hall, with violet-scented soap and soft, white towels. But Ainderby was a fairy-tale palace, set in that other world, something they had talked about on winter evenings.

"Tell me, Mam," Sarah would plead, snuggling close. "Tell me about Ainderby."

The Ball had been one of her favourites, she recalled; the coming of age of Ainderby's eldest son and half the gentry in Lancashire dancing the night away.

"*Real* gentry," her mother insisted. "Gentlemen born, not mill-owners."

Her mother's voice had been soft and low. It was the way you learned to speak, it seemed, when you entered service in a gentleman's house. Mary Makin had been a parlourmaid and worn soft boots and long, warm frocks and starched aprons, bleached white. And all the servants at Ainderby slept in beds with counterpanes on them and nobody, not even the tweenies, set a foot out of bed until six-thirty.

Half-past six. By that time, Sarah thought dully, she had walked the mile to Low Clough mill and put in thirty minutes work.

She hated the weaving-shed. Since she could remember she had wanted to work at a great house like Ainderby, but such positions went to the favoured few. Most Hollinsdyke women ended up in one or another of the mills around and wedded a mill-worker and produced un-wanted bairns to work in the mills, too.

"I'll not get married," Sarah whispered, cutting savagely at the bread loaf. "The man hasn't been born who'll entice me into misery."

For that was all marriage was. A mean wage and a mean little house. To marry was to change one weary way for another. Best stay as she was and strive for better things, hope that one day Luke Holroyd would get his comeuppance, that his mill would fall down, that a lady would drive up in a carriage and take her off to work in a house like Ainderby.

"Cut a cob for me, lass."

Startled, Sarah saw Caleb standing in the door-way.

"You're up early, Father. Not poorly, are you?"

"I'm right enough, but I couldn't sleep," Caleb nodded.

"I've a mind to go to Moor Top woods, see if the celandines are out. We're into March now.

March. Springtime. Sarah hadn't noticed. There were no seasons in the Three-streets, no trees or birds or flowers. The chimneys that dominated the town shut out the sky with their smoke and spread a blanket over the sun. Only if she walked to the hills that ringed Hollinsdyke around could she feel grass beneath her feet and breathe air that was sweet and cool. Now, for all his misfortune, she envied her father. He would spend the day in the woods and fields, searching for celandines to make into salve and wild pansies for eye-wash. Local folk relied on Caleb's lotions and potions. His mugwort tea was without equal for an upset stomach and his wood-sorrel syrup had soothed most of the street's teething babies. Caleb had even been known to cure warts, when the mood was on him, thought it was for his raspberry-leaf infusion that he was most famed, and the pregnant women who drank it swore it dulled their labour pangs.

"It's a fair step to Moor Top," Sarah cautioned.

"I'll take it easy. I've got all the time in the world."

11

There was a note of bitterness in his voice, but she chose to ignore it.

"I'll take Billy-Boy a couple of pieces," she murmured, reaching for the dripping-jar.

"Aye, lass. Likely he'll be hungry."

Billy-Boy was always hungry. Billy-Boy was a workhouse child, abandoned as a baby on the chapel steps. Now he was nine and worked in the weaving-shed at Low Clough, running errands, sweeping floors, cleaning machines. Against her better judgement, Sarah had come to care for him and the child sensed that reluctant affection, clinging to it jealously, for it was the only tenderness he had ever known. Each morning he waited for her at the mill gate, wearing boots too small and trousers too large, his fair hair cropped short, brown eyes large in a pale, thin face. Seeing him there like a small, unwanted puppy aroused feelings in Sarah she had never thought to admit to and she would take his hand in hers and walk with him to the hot damp weaving-shed.

All Low Clough was damp. It had been standing for a hundred years and was fast falling into disrepair. Once Luke Holroyd had been a spinner in that very mill and had managed, though God alone knew how, to rise above himself and buy the place. It had been the talk of Hollinsdyke for months with everybody saying that here at last would be a mill-owner who cared.

But he had done nothing to improve it, forgetting the men he'd worked with, as easy as falling off a log. Nobody in Hollinsdyke liked him, yet they allowed him grudging respect for what he had achieved. He was the master now, so they tipped their caps to him as he passed in his carriage. It was the way of the world. No use fighting it.

Sarah wrapped her midday bread in a cloth then filled her water-bottle at the backyard pump. Imagine water in taps. Imagine a world where there were no mill-masters, no orphans like Billy-Boy or men like her father. Imagine clean streets and clean air and sunlight.

"I hate you, Luke Holroyd," Sarah whispered. "I'll never own you've got the right to set yourself up as God Almighty, thumb your nose at the law, work children for a pittance."

But at least he couldn't employ a bairn under nine years old, now. And he had to see to it that the children in his mill got three hours schooling a day, for this was 1870 and the world's slow conscience was stirring. Black slaves were a thing of the past. Soon, maybe, there'd be no white ones either.

When would he come, she sighed, the long-promised Messiah who would fight for their rights? One day, happen, when she was too old to care. And until then she had four looms to tend and a sick father to feed. So stop your imagining, Sarah Makin, she chided silently; stop sighing for what might have been . . .

"I'm off, then." She draped her shawl over her

head and shoulders and pinned it firmly beneath her chin. "Mind what you're about on Moor Top. Don't go tiring yourself."

"I'll think on. And watch yourself, an' all."

They didn't kiss. Words of caution and grave admonitions were the only affections that passed between them. There was no love now in the little house in Canal Street. Just a kind of hopeless caring. And it was better that way, Sarah accepted, slamming the door behind her. Loving laid hearts bare and weakened resolve. Loving was a luxury in the Three-streets.

It was still dark and lamplight streamed like a beacon through the open doorway of the end house in Tinker's Row. An open door on a cold morning signalled trouble and Sarah slowed her steps and called:

"Anything the matter, Liza?"

"Eh, lass. I've been waiting for you to come along." Liza Nuttall grasped Sarah's arm. "Can you slip back and fetch your father? I'm worried half to death." She nodded toward the corner of the room where her husband lay in the shadow, coughing quietly. "He's gone on and on, all night, and now he's spitting blood. Happen Caleb can help — mix him a dose?"

But Sarah had seen consumption before. "There's nothing my father can do for that," she retorted grimly. "It's a doctor you need now, Liza."

But doctors cost money. They even insisted on cash in advance in places like Tinker's Row. A

14

shilling it would cost and Liza was penniless.

"I'll lend you the money. I get paid tonight," Sarah offered rashly, knowing it could never be repaid. "And don't fret," she comforted. "I'll call at the doctor's on my way in. When he comes, tell him Sarah Makin'll pay."

The church clock chimed three times the quarter. Fifteen minutes to starting time! She picked up her skirts and ran.

The yard gates were shut when she arrived, breathless, at Low Clough.

"You're late. Three minutes," the timekeeper pronounced, pushing a book at her and a stub of pencil.

"But I've been for the doctor!" Sarah protested.

"Three minutes late. Three pence fined," the man persisted. "Better sign sharpish, or it'll be four!"

She reached through the gate and scribbled her name in the Fines Book.

"Rot your clogs!" she flung, as he let her in. Deep in trouble already and the day hardly begun!

The overlooker stared meaningfully when Sarah clattered into the weaving-shed, but made no comment for she usually kept good time. No sense in causing a rumpus. Caleb's lass had a peppery temper, when roused.

Billy-Boy smiled, relieved to see her, peering

15

anxiously at her apron pocket for the tell-tale bulge that meant bread and dripping at dinner-time.

Sarah threw aside her shawl then abandoned herself to the noise of the shed. She had long ago ceased to fight it. Now there were even times when she hardly noticed it. At first the thunderous roar made her afraid and she had wondered what would happen if ever she had cause to scream. No one would hear her. If the chimney-stack fell, none would know save those it fell on, for the crash and clatter of a hundred looms would drown the blast of the Last Call, when it came!

She smiled at Billy-Boy and mouthed 'Hullo', setting her looms into motion, checking bobbins and shuttles, breathing deeply to calm the anger that bubbled inside her. Three pennies fined and a shilling to Liza for the doctor! Precious little left to last the week on. Oh, damn Luke Holroyd! Damn all mill-masters!

She looked up and saw the nodding heads of Poll Clegg and Belle Birtle. They were talking about her, gloating over her fine. Belle was a troublemaker with a quiet way of talking that made everybody listen. Belle put words into the mouths of others, then sat back with pleasure to enjoy the upset. She didn't care that Sarah was watching the exaggerated moving of her lips, reading the words as clearly as she read a printed page.

Sarah stared dully across the shed. Belle, she

decided, was in the mood for a bit of trouble to start the day with. She turned her back on the taunting face. Let her find it somewhere else. Sarah Makin had had bother enough for one day!

But Billy-Boy was not so cautious. Confronting the gossiping women he took up the cause.

"You're talking about my Sarah," he stormed, his small face flushed. "Sarah's my friend and you're a wicked old woman, Belle Birtle!"

"Why you — you cheeky little shaver!"

Poll's hand flashed out, catching the child a blow to his ear, sending him sprawling. Belle smiled, well satisfied.

Anger blazed red on Sarah's cheeks. Jamming her hands on her hips she marched into battle.

"Do that again!" she challenged, sticking out her chin.

She had thought her show of protest would be the end of it, that Poll would withdraw. She hadn't bargained for the stinging slap that was delivered to the side of her face.

"Aaaah! Why — you . . ."

Honour demanded that Sarah should retaliate. If she didn't, there would be no living with Belle Birtle's smugness. She returned the blow with venom.

"That'll be all, now!"

The overlooker was quick to drag the gasping women apart, marching them roughly toward the doors.

"Fighting in t'mill isn't allowed. You should

17

both know that!"

Fighting in the shed was dangerous too. It could end in one or the other of the participants being hurled against a moving machine and that was a messy business, to say the least. The yard was the place for such things. And they'd be fined a shilling apiece for brawling, so why not let them get their money's worth? he reasoned.

"Out! If you've got to fight, then do it in the gutter!" he bawled, slamming the doors on them. And may they claw each other to pieces, for all he cared!

David Holroyd arrived at Low Clough in time to bear witness to the set-to. At first he was taken aback, wondering what he should do. It would, he supposed, be wisest to ignore it. No one in his right mind tried to come between snarling dogs and the same applied to fighting women. It would be a brave man who got himself embroiled in that heaving tangle of black-stockinged legs and thrusting, steel-tipped clogs.

And then he saw the face of the young one, the face of the girl who walked barefoot on Moor Top hill with the wind in her long, black curls and her fine-boned face held high to the sun. He'd seen her there often, remembering her beauty, wondering who she was. Now, sadly, he knew. She was a Low Clough weaver, fighting in his father's yard and getting the worst of it too.

"Stop it! Stop it at once, I say!"

The authority in his voice surprised him and that the brawling should instantly cease.

"You!" he jerked, glaring at Poll with all the dignity he could gather. "Get back to your work, and *you*," he jabbed his walking-stick at Sarah. "Come with me!"

Dejectedly Sarah rose to her feet and dusted down her skirts. Fighting was one thing; getting caught at it by the master's son was another. At the best it would be another fine and at the worst it could bring dismissal. Panting with exertion, her head throbbing with pain she followed despondently, remembering her father's words.

'That temper'll be the ruination of you, my lass. Mark my words if it won't!'

Now her father had been proved right and she was deep in trouble. Backed up by Belle Birtle, they would believe what Poll Clegg told them. Poll was a valuable six-loom weaver. Poll who was never absent, never late, would get the benefit of the doubt, Sarah argued silently and Belle Birtle would laugh for a week at the trouble she'd caused.

"What is your name?" David Holroyd asked, closing the door of his office behind him. "And why were you fighting?"

"My name is Sarah Makin," she said slowly, tilting her chin, trying to speak the way her mother had spoken. "I'm a four-loom weaver and I always make my yardage," she added defiantly.

"And?"

"And I was fighting because Poll Clegg slapped

Billy-Boy. He's a child. She'd no right to do it!"

A warning bell rang stridently in her head, telling her to stop while there was yet time, but she was angry now; she'd say her piece, by Lud, and go down fighting!

"Do you ever give a thought to the children in your mill, Mister David? Do you ever stop to think how cheaply your money is made?"

She paused, breathless, and looked into his face, seeing for the first time the clean-shaven cheeks, the deep blue eyes that looked calmly into her own.

This was the end. She had gone too far. Drymouthed, suddenly afraid, she stared back, waiting for the blow to fall.

"Sit down, Sarah," came the quiet reply. "Please?"

Startled, she did as he asked. Sarah, he'd called her. "Please?" he'd said.

So that was his game! He was the master's son and she a mill-girl and a mill-girl was easy pickings! Oh, but she knew all about mill-owner's sons and the girls they'd had their way with then left at the workhouse door, their trouble hidden beneath their pinnies.

Lowering her eyes, she began to think desperately of a way out.

Perhaps if she told him she was sorry for what she had said he would let her off with a fine. It would be better than losing her job? Maybe, if she was to squeeze out a tear or two, put on an act, it would help. It was worth a try. She had nothing to lose. Tremulously she sighed and raised her face to his.

"I'm sorry for what I said, sir . . ."

David stared fascinated at the girl with the brown, pleading eyes. She was far more beautiful than he had first realised; even with her tangled hair and grimy face and a bruise on her cheek that grew redder as he watched.

"I'm sorry you had to say it," he heard himself retort. "Is it so very awful, working at Low Clough?"

Anger flamed afresh inside her. Just one week in that shed and he wouldn't need to ask! She opened her lips to fling scorn into his face again, then remembered the danger wasn't over. Breathing deeply, blinking a tear from the corner of her eye, she whispered:

"It's worse than awful. I'd do *anything* to get away from Low Clough."

"But where would you go, Sarah, except to another mill?"

"I could go to a place like Ainderby," she retorted. "Be a parlourmaid. Work for a gentleman and be treated decent."

"A *servant?*"

"Oh, yes. I'd like that."

She lifted her head and he saw real animation in her face. A servant, indeed! She was worth better than that! Caution cast aside, he said,

"Tell me about yourself, Sarah. How old are you? Where do you live?"

"I'm twenty and I live in Canal Street."

"And are you married?" She wasn't wearing a ring, but that meant nothing.

"Married? That I'm *not!*"

"And have you brothers, or sisters?"

"No, sir. There's just me and father. Mam died of typhoid when I was twelve, then father got lamed in the mill."

She said it, he thought, as if such tragedies were commonplace, a part of life to be accepted without question.

"Can you read and write, Sarah Makin?"

"Course I can," she said scornfully. "And figure too."

"So you went to school?"

"Until I was twelve. I'd have been as good as Maggie Ormerod if I could have stayed on," she added hastily.

"Miss Ormerod who teaches the mill apprentices, you mean?"

"Aye," Sarah nodded, amused. *Miss* Ormerod indeed! Why, Maggie was from the same mould as herself and lived in Albert Court, not a spit away. But Maggie had done well at school and been singled out by the Minister to teach Luke Holroyd's mill children. Maggie went to her work in a bonnet and gloves.

"And can you add and subtract and multiply?"

"Set me some sums, and I'll show you," she challenged eagerly, wondering for all that what sums and schooling had to do with fighting.

"I'll take your word for it," he said quietly, wondering what madness was putting ideas into his mind. Sarah Makin was a weaver and used to nothing else. Wouldn't it be fairer to leave her where she was, tell her to mend her ways and send her back to the sheds?

But she had long fascinated him. There was a wildness about her that excited him as none of the young ladies of his acquaintance had ever done.

"Sarah," he smiled. "There is a position for a lady-clerk in the counting-house, here at Low Clough. Would you like it?"

Would she like it?

In that instant Sarah's world exploded deliriously about her. Stars cascaded before her eyes and a thousand mill-hooters shrieked inside her head.

But there had to be a catch to it. Nobody did anything for nothing, least of all a Holroyd. Yet here was the chance she had been waiting for, the chance to get out of the shed, to better herself.

"*Me?*" she whispered.

"Why not?" he retorted, delighted by her reaction. "Unless you're determined to be a servant, that is?"

"How much?" she countered. "What'll you pay?"

"Ten and six a week. Eight o'clock start."

"And no fines?"

"No fines — well, not unless you're caught fighting again."

"Then it's a bargain," she replied solemnly,

holding out her hand. "When do I start?"

"Monday morning. Report to Mr Dinwiddie."

He took her hand in his as was the way with sealing a bargain and suddenly the full realisation of his rashness struck him. He'd been an utter fool and his father, when he heard about it, would tell him he was out of his mind. Usually he bowed to all his father's wishes, but in this, he vowed, he would stand firm. Sarah Makin fascinated him and this time he would do as he pleased. He would have her near him and nothing his father or Dinwiddie might say would change it!

Head spinning, heart thumping, Sarah clattered across the yard to the shed.

"Imagine!" she exulted, the full force of her good fortune hitting her for the first time. "A lady-clerk!" Imagine going to work in the daylight. Imagine Sarah Makin in a bonnet and gloves and slim, soft boots.

"Oh, my Lord," she whispered, because she didn't have any boots. She had never worn anything but clogs.

The noise of the shed stretched out to meet her, eager to enfold her, claim her back. But it didn't matter. After Saturday the sheds would be nothing more than a miserable memory. No more noise, no more weariness, no more fines. Come Sunday she would be free of it all.

Straightening her shoulders and throwing back her head she gave a great shout of joy.

Who cared about boots? There'd be time

enough to worry about such things tomorrow. This moment, this wonderful, *wonderful* moment, the only thing that mattered was Belle Birtle's face.

"Just wait until I tell her!" Sarah thrilled. "Only wait!"

It seemed, suddenly, as if the sun was shining and she was walking barefoot on Moor Top hill, with every bird in creation singing fit to burst.

Sarah Makin was on her way up in the world and by old Lud she'd show them!

But her joy was short-lived for it was obvious, as she neared her home that night, that death had walked the Three-streets. At every window of every house curtains had been closed in unspoken respect.

"Was it Will Nuttall?" Sarah asked, filling her bowl from the broth-pan that hung above the kitchen fire.

"Aye. Two hours gone."

"And how is Liza taking it?" No use grieving for the dead, Sarah reasoned. Best by far to have a care for the living. "I'll go round and see her."

"I wouldn't. There's folk a-plenty there, weeping and wailing," Caleb supplied. "I took her a draft for her nerves . . ."

"How will she manage?" Sarah hazarded.

"God alone knows," he shrugged. "Liza's proud. She'll not plead poverty."

"Then I'd best take the tin round."

This morning Liza hadn't had the price of the

doctor in her pocket and it was unlikely things could have changed meantime. Best make haste with a collection while there was still some money about, Sarah decided, gratified that Will Nuttall had had the good sense to choose pay-day on which to breathe his last.

No one in the Three-streets refused a contribution and money rattled into Sarah's tin. At the Black Bull ale-house, unusually busy with Friday night spenders, the landlord gave Sarah permission to collect, opening his drawer, taking out a shilling. Will Nuttall hadn't been a drinking man, he reasoned, but doubtless Liza would buy the funeral ale from the Bull.

"My condolences to Mrs Nuttall," he said.

"Aye. I'll tell her you gave," Sarah acknowledged dryly.

"Here, lass!" Someone tugged at her shawl and Sarah spun round, tin extended. A man held a sixpenny piece aloft. "Who's it for?"

"Who's asking?" she demanded bluntly. The man was a stranger, to be treated with caution.

"Robey Midwinter." The reply was equally brusque.

"Are you from the Parish Relief?"

"That I'm not! And don't worry — I'll not let on you're collecting," he assured her, dropping the coin into the tin. "Who's dead?" he asked again.

"Will Nuttall," Sarah supplied reluctantly.

"A mill-worker?"

"Aye. From the card-room at Low Clough, before the coughing took a hold."

"Luke Holroyd's mill? And how much will *he* be giving?"

"Nothing," Sarah replied flatly. "Mister Holroyd doesn't believe in charity."

"But surely it was his cotton-dust that caused the trouble?"

"Happen it was," she snapped, suddenly angered by the stranger's questioning. "But Luke Holroyd'll not lose any sleep over that!" Confronted, he would swear it had been Will's fault for breathing it in. "He'll not care!"

"Then he should be made to care!"

Sarah shrugged. The man wanted to know too much. Let him find the answers to his questions elsewhere.

"Then maybe you're the right one to do it, Robey Midwinter!" she flung, turning away abruptly, annoyed with herself for noticing that his shoulders were straight and broad and his mocking eyes black as the night.

"Happen I am," he whispered to her indignant retreating back. "Happen I am, at that!"

It wasn't until almost midnight that Sarah was able to tell her father about the goings-on at the mill.

"Just like that?" Caleb questioned. "Young Holroyd catches you fighting then offers you a job in the counting-house? Is it likely?"

"It's the sober truth," Sarah retorted. "I

thought you'd be pleased."

"I might have been if there was any sense in it. A Holroyd giving favours? What's behind it?"

"Nothing's behind it, father!" She jumped angrily to her feet then shook her head in despair. Since his accident her father had looked on the world with distrust. Nothing pleased him nowadays. If Luke Holroyd were to fall head first into the workhouse midden, it wouldn't bring so much as a smile to her father's lips, she thought wearily. Yet maybe his suspicions were not entirely without foundation? No use denying she had used her wiles, wept a little. But who could blame her for that? Her job had been at risk and, if David Holroyd had got wrong ideas into his head, then that was his fault!

"You've tired yourself out, tramping all that way to Moor Top," she scolded, giving way to compassion. She found it impossible to be angry for long and a wave of pity for her father washed over her, just as it did when she looked at Billy-Boy. She had to try to be more patient. Once Caleb had been a strong, well set-up man. Small wonder then that sometimes he should give way to despair.

"There was a stranger in the Black Bull tonight," she offered cheerfully. "Asked a lot of questions, but he gave me a sixpence for Liza's tin."

"Aye — that'll be Robey."

"You know him?" Trust her father to keep

such news to himself.

Caleb sucked at his empty pipe and stared into the fire looking almost, Sarah thought, as if he were sorry to have told her.

"He's taken a bed at Ormerod's," he said eventually.

"Since when has Maggie's ma taken in lodgers?"

"Since this morning. I met Robey on the hill road, on my way up to the tops. He asked if I knew of any lodgings and we talked awhile."

"And where is he from? What's he doing here?"

"He didn't say. To hear him talk he's been to most parts, though what there is in Hollinsdyke for the likes of him is beyond me."

"Happen he's looking for work?"

"Happen."

Caleb shrugged and jammed the stem of his pipe between his teeth again, indicating that the conversation was over. Anything else she wanted to know about Robey Midwinter, Sarah conceded, she would have to learn for herself.

But weren't there more important things in her life? Men were of small concern to a girl who was busy getting on in the world. And, besides, Robey Midwinter was far too proud, much too handsome. And his eyes were full of mockery and mischief.

His arrogance she could accept, his good looks she could shrug aside, but a stranger who asked questions was altogether another matter. So best forget him?

Sarah bid farewell to the weaving-shed at Low Clough with undisguised pleasure. Every hour of that last day had seemed to stretch itself into a lifetime but now she was free of it she could feel nothing but relief. Saying goodbye to Billy-Boy caused the only sadness, for the child had clung to her, crying quietly, begging her not to leave him.

"But I shall only be across the yard, in the counting-house," she whispered. "And I'll wave to you, from the window."

"You'll forget me, Sarah."

But she wouldn't forget him. That was why she was on her way now, to see Maggie Ormerod. Maggie was Billy Boy's teacher and it seemed a good idea, Sarah reasoned, to ask her to keep an eye on the child, tell her at once if he got sick. She chose to ignore the faint voice of her conscience that suggested the visit to Albert Court might not be entirely concerned with the child's welfare. She really wasn't interested in Ormerod's new lodger. Admitted, he made her curious, but the tallness of him, his blatant masculinity and his tantalising smile meant absolutely nothing, she insisted yet again.

Maggie greeted her warmly.

"Come in, Sarah lass. It's grand to see you."

Plump, pretty Maggie, with corn-gold hair, an angel smile and a mind free from any kind of malice.

"Sit you down," she smiled, setting the kettle

to boil, arranging tea-cups on a tray.

Maggie had pretty manners. She could pass for a lady any day of the week, Sarah acknowledged, noting the long full skirt, the white, high-necked blouse and soft, highly-polished boots. Sarah Makin could do a lot worse than copy the school-teacher. Sarah Makin could —

Robey Midwinter strode into the kitchen as if the place were his own, crashing into Sarah's daydreams, sending a reluctant flush to her cheeks. But she collected herself sufficiently to incline her head when Maggie introduced them, making no mention of their meeting in the Black Bull, pretending surprise that he should be there.

"You're a weaver, aren't you, at Low Clough?" he demanded abruptly of Sarah. "What are conditions like?"

"Like anywhere else," she replied, taken aback. Questions. Always questions.

"I heard they were bad," he insisted flatly. "Talk has it that Luke Holroyd's mill is the worst in these parts, and damp too."

"It's damp," Sarah acknowledged, "but show me the cotton-mill that isn't? If you knew anything at all about it, you'd not need to be told that cotton needs moisture in the weaving."

"Oh, I know about cotton-mills, all right," he flung, "and woollen-mills too. And I can tell you about coal-mines and tin-mines —"

He broke off abruptly, shrugging his shoulders . . .

"Robey's a deep thinker," Maggie interrupted

31

gently. "Things bother him. Tell him about your good fortune, Sarah. Cheer him up."

Sarah hadn't meant to be flippant about it, turn it all into a joke, but a desire to impress Robey Midwinter arose strong inside her and the mischief in her soul urged her on. She took the centre of the floor as if it were a stage.

"Oh, I thought I was in for the sack!" she gasped, laughter dancing in her eyes. "There we were, Poll Clegg and me, rolling in the muck. And wasn't it just my luck to get caught?"

Impishly delighted by the sound of her own voice, Sarah gave a dramatic account of her pleading, her crocodile tears and David Holroyd's gullibility.

"Fell for it, he did — daft as a brush!"

Then she gave an exaggerated impression of the mill-owner's son, mimicking his voice, turning it all into a farce; a farce, she realised suddenly, that wasn't funny.

No one was laughing. At any other time Maggie would have been amused, taken her performance with a pinch of salt and told her, smiling, she was a right caution. Maggie understood her, but not Robey Midwinter. Slab-faced, he watched her antics, waiting until her last whispered word hung still on the uneasy air before saying,

"And I suppose it makes you proud? Is that the way to better yourself — simpering and smiling and degrading your womanhood? Oh, there's nothing like a bit of lick-spittling to the master's son, is there, especially if he's pretty to look at and has an eye for a mill-girl that's easy? You did well for yourself, Sarah Makin. It'll be interesting to see the price you pay for your grovelling!"

It would have been wisest, Sarah knew, to have bowed out gracefully, to have left well alone and allowed his sneers to ride over her. After all, she had gone too far; she'd asked for it. But his eyes were mocking her again and anger was quickly replacing her dismay.

"All right — so it was wrong of me to do what I did," she flung. "But what would you have done in my place? I was sick of the shed and so would you be too! You've never stood on a mill floor until your legs turned to lead and you don't know what it's like to work in that noise, day after day. So don't presume to judge me, Robey Midwinter!"

Snatching up her shawl, near blinded by tears, she slammed out of the house, walking blindly, rage and shame writhing inside her. She'd made a fool of herself in front of Robey Midwinter. She'd been impetuous again, rushing in without thought like she always did, and this time the joke had misfired. Her father was right. One day her unthinking ways would land her in real trouble and she would spend the rest of her life being sorry for it.

Why couldn't she be more like Maggie? Maggie was of mill-stock like everyone else in the Three-streets, yet she had a way about her that commanded respect. But it was all Robey Midwinter's fault, rot his clogs! She would never have done it, but for him! There was something about him that disturbed her, turned her into a show-off. Why had he needed to come to Hollinsdyke and how long would he be staying?

But maybe tomorrow he would be on his way again, she reasoned hopefully, for he'd soon find there was no work in Hollinsdyke for strangers who asked too many questions.

Mollified, she looked upwards to the hills. Oh, be damned to Robey Midwinter! Maggie Ormerod could have him, and welcome!

Sarah's temper was spent and her natural optimism restored when finally she reached the budding trees of Moor Top woods. Kicking aside her clogs, pulling off her stockings, she thrust her feet into the beck that flowed, ice-cold, down the hillside. Here, where there was nothing to stop her reaching up and touching God, the grass was soft and green and the pale Spring sun shone gently. Here, high above the town, all was stillness and, if she didn't look down, there would be nothing at all to remind her that Hollinsdyke existed.

Leaning back on her elbows, closing her eyes, she breathed deeply. Tomorrow work began in Luke Holroyd's counting-house. Soon she would be able to buy soft leather boots and dainty gloves. And she would try, she really would try, to think before she spoke and keep a hold on her temper, be more like Maggie.

"Good-afternoon, Miss Makin."

Sarah's eyes flew open and, startled, remained open, gazing upward with dismay. Oh my goodness, she'd done it again; got herself caught with skirts above her knees and up to the ankles in beck water.

"Mr David!"

David Holroyd smiled and squatted beside her, searching his brain for something to say, wondering why the sight of her tied his tongue so.

"Not in church, then?"

"No, sir." Of course she wasn't in church!

"Do you often come here?"

"Only on Sundays and nights, if it's light." All other days she worked — didn't he know that?

"You surprised me, Sarah — meeting you here, that is." Liar. He had come here especially.

"You surprised *me*, Mr David." Gravely she held out a dripping foot.

She was very beautiful, he conceded, fixing a picture in his mind to take away with him. Barefoot Sarah, with flowing hair and cheeks whipped rosy by the wind.

And there was a waywardness about her that sent excitement thrashing through him, set him searching for words as if he were a pimply youth.

He wanted more than anything to stay and talk. Tomorrow, at the mill, it might not be so easy.

Unbidden, a fleeting vision of another Sarah flashed before him; Sarah in velvet and satin, with silk stockings clinging to her ankles and

35

dainty shoes on her pretty pink feet. And it was useless to deny it any longer — he wanted her for himself. She was exquisite. She set his blood racing yet he couldn't even offer his arm, walk back with her to the outskirts of town. To have done that would have proclaimed, to a mill-girl's way of thinking, that they were walking out and pledged to wedlock. There was a strange, strict code of behaviour among the working classes, he acknowledged, that was almost prudish. Best tread carefully. Sarah Makin was a fey creature; one wrong move and he'd lose her.

Abruptly he raised his hat. "Bid you good-day, ma'am."

Sarah watched him go, her forehead creased. He had called her Miss Makin and raised his hat and if she could only forget he was a Holroyd she was sure she could find him very agreeable.

But mill-owner's sons needed a lot of watching. They were like their elders who had got rich because they'd never done anything for nothing. David Holroyd had taken her out of the mill and her father had demanded to know what was behind it. And Robey Midwinter had given his unasked opinion, telling her she would have to pay.

But would she? Only wait, and she would show them all who would be doing the paying! David Holroyd wouldn't have things all his own way and as for Master Midwinter — why, she wouldn't care if she never saw him again! In fact, there was only one thing about him that bothered her. He irritated her so much that she couldn't get him out of her mind!

She shook her head, wondering why it was that suddenly her life should have become so vaguely complicated, why it seemed she was waiting, breathless, for something to happen. It was a feeling she could not explain. It frightened and excited her at one and the same time. It was rooted in the past yet seemed to be beckoning her on to a turbulent tomorrow. And bound up in it were David Holroyd and Robey Midwinter; the one she mistrusted and the other she disliked.

Where in heaven's name was it all to end?

Two

"Tell me about the counting-house." Billy-Boy's voice was hushed with reverence.

Sarah looked thoughtfully at her last piece of bread then handed it to the child.

"It's very nice, Billy. Very genteel . . ."

She puckered her forehead, searching for words, for the counting-house at Low Clough mill had proved to be something of a disappointment and not the holy of holies she had imagined it to be. The long-legged desks were old and worn, the wooden floors bare and the smell of musty paper sickened the air.

"Of course, it's nothing like the weaving-shed. As I was saying this morning to Mr Dobson —"

Joshua Dobson was the gentlest of men, and patient to a fault, for which blessing Sarah had quickly found reason to be thankful. The bothers that beset a lady-clerk were beyond belief. The mastering of four temperamental looms had been child's play compared to the pitfalls and man-traps of the Order-by-Post department. But give her time and she would get the better of that too.

"As I was saying to Mr Dobson when we had our tea and biscuits —"

"*Biscuits*, Sarah?"

"Yes, indeed! Currant biscuits and tea in china cups."

Such pretty little cups, thin as could be and sprinkled with pink rosebuds. They had belonged to his mother, Mr Dobson explained, and Sarah had flushed with pride, sticking out her little finger in a lady-like gesture as she drank.

She was well aware of the existence of such luxuries, of course. They had used china cups at Ainderby. Every day. Imagine such a thing.

"And is it better than working in the shed?"

"It is, Billy-Boy. It is," she nodded, begging silent forgiveness for such a downright untruth. Indeed her first impressions of the counting-house had been those of distinct hostility. Two gentleman clerks with slicked-down hair and hurt expressions had gazed right through her, and as for Mr Dinwiddie! Well, he had been most un-friendly, declaring loudly that as soon as Mr Holroyd got himself back from Manchester there'd be trouble! He'd have an explanation, Dinwiddie would, or he'd know the reason why! And as for Mr David! *That* young man had taken leave of his senses, bringing a mill-lass into the counting-house without so much as a by-your-leave!

After which show of protest Dinwiddie had retreated to his office, wondering out loud what the world was coming to. Thank the good Lord, Sarah had sighed, for Mr Dobson. He at least had been kind.

"Come in Miss Makin, do. I'm glad you're here."

Small and elderly and much overworked, his

welcome had been genuine and Sarah warmed with remembered pride at being so addressed.

Painstakingly he had explained the workings of the Order-by-Post department.

"It was Mr David's idea, you see. The country housewife likes being able to order her linen by letter. The Master and Mr Dinwiddie were both against it, at first. New-fangled, they said it was and doomed to fail. But it's doing well — so well that sometimes I can't keep up with all the invoicing and packing." He smiled timidly. "I was glad when I heard you were coming. Trouble is," he sighed, "Mr David didn't think to tell Mr Dinwiddie about you and I'm afraid the gentleman is somewhat piqued. But I dare say it'll all get sorted out before long."

The counting-house at Low Clough mill, Sarah discovered, consisted of four rooms. One for Luke Holroyd, one for his son; a large, musty room where the clerks worked and a small cubbyhole into which Mr Dinwiddie retreated in times of stress. The Order-by-Post department, being something of a novelty, was housed in a storeroom at the end of the corridor. Its window was very small, its ceiling very high, its walls a drab green. But the room had the benefit of a small, iron firegrate on the hob of which Mr Dobson's little black kettle bubbled constantly.

"You'll feel strange at first, Miss Sarah, but they leave us alone, this being Mr David's experiment, so to speak," he smiled, handing her a cup of tea, offering a biscuit from a tin with the Prince Consort's picture on the lid. Joshua Dobson's kindness had cheered Sarah enormously and before long she was singing happily as she packed pillow ticking, tea-towels and un-bleached sheeting into neat, brown-paper parcels.

The knocking-off hooter blared and Sarah looked up, surprised that dinnertime had come without further interference from Mr Dinwiddie. Picking up her bundle she hurried to the mill-yard, suddenly lonely for Billy-Boy.

"Said I wouldn't forget you, didn't I?" she smiled, unwrapping her bread, giving him half. She had tried not to love Billy-Boy. Loving people, gathering them close, was a luxury she could not afford. If she was to get on in the world she had to be free, so that when her chances came she could move on without encumbrances, without regret. But for all that she had come to care for the child. Against her better judgement she had let him gentle his way into her heart. She felt protective towards him, responsible for his well-being. He was the child she would never bear, she supposed, for marriage did not rate high in her plans. Bringing innocent babes into the world was downright sinful. There aught to be a law against it.

The hooter invaded her thoughts with lungs of brass.

"It's one o'clock, Billy. Be off to school with you." She hugged the child briefly. "And learn your lessons like a good lad."

Dipping into the pocket of her skirt she took out the biscuit she had slipped there earlier.

"Here you are. I saved it for you."

The child regarded the unexpected treat with awe.

"Go on, lad. Eat it up afore somebody takes it off you!"

"You'll come again tomorrow, Sarah?"

"I'll come. Promise."

She watched him go, shaking her head with disbelief that a child could be treated so. Billy-Boy lived his life between the confines of the mill and the workhouse orphanage; six hours in the weaving-shed and three hours schooling. Always ragged, always hungry. Nine years old and ninety years wise.

Oh imagine, Sarah yearned, a world without unhappiness. Imagine a world without hunger or cold, without mill-owners or workhouse-masters, a world of rosebud china and water in taps.

But Maggie was kind to the bairns in the mill-school, Sarah owned, and made sure her class-room was warm and bright as she could make it. Nor did she, in her compassion, ever awaken a child who fell asleep, exhausted, over his slate.

Tonight, Sarah decided, she would call on Maggie. There were matters to discuss with her friend — matters of importance, like the buying of shoes and how to brighten up her clothes. Before this her appearance had mattered little. Mill-girls wore skirts and blouses and pinafores and to have tried to ape their betters would never have occurred to them.

But Sarah Makin had gone up in the world. A lady-clerk wore a cape and bonnet and shoes or button-boots. Small wonder they had looked down their noses at her, Sarah sighed. There had been the stamp of the Three-streets on her and it wouldn't do.

But come next reckoning-day she would be rich. There would even be money over to spend on herself and then she would show them! She'd walk the Three-streets as proud as Lucifer and as for that bothersome Robey Midwinter — well, just let him wait! Next time he sneered at her she would draw herself up, all haughty-like and look at him down her nose. He'd not get her flustered again, be sure of that!

She shook her head, angry with herself for even thinking about him. But he bothered her. Try as she would, she could not get him out of her mind.

Who was he? Why had he come? But such matters had to wait. The hooter had gone and it simply would not do to be late back. Not on her first day. Not ever.

Luke Holroyd had spent a very profitable morning at the Cotton Exchange, eaten a delicious cold luncheon at his Manchester club and returned to Low Clough well pleased with himself. Then, just as he had been about to settle down for a doze, the counting-house manager burst into his office.

"I'll have to have words, Mister Holroyd, for I'm fair beside myself with grievance!"

"What is it, Albert?" the mill-master clucked testily. "Can't young David see to it?"

"That he can't, Master. It's on account of Mr David I'm here. He's the cause of it — him and that lass!"

"What lass?" Luke sat bolt upright in his chair. "What's our David been up to, then?"

"He's gone behind my back, that's what. Without so much as a word to me he takes a lass from t' weaving-shed and sets her up as a clerk. I wouldn't care, but lasses like her upset the tone of the place. Only last week she was brawling in t' yard and ever since she's come she's been singing at the top of her voice and clattering up and down the passage. I tell you, Mr Holroyd, you'll not have a floorboard left come reckoning-day, with them clog-irons of hers!"

Luke Holroyd sighed annoyance, his mellow mood gone. Albert Dinwiddie's petulant outbursts were enough to cope with; he could do well without young David's adding to the bother. Banging loudly on the partition wall, he nodded placatingly.

"All right, Albert. Say no more. Let's see what the lad has to say for himself!"

When David Holroyd answered his father's summons he was greeted tersely.

"Now then — what about this lass you've taken on?"

44

"Josh Dobson's assistant? Sarah Makin?"

"Makin? Caleb's lass, is she?"

"Yes, Father."

"Aye, and without so much as a by-your-leave, Mr David! Without telling me!" Dinwiddie interrupted. "Undermined my authority, you have . . ."

"You surprise me, Mr Dinwiddie." David raised an eyebrow. "As I recall, you said you wanted nothing to do with the Order-by-Post department. 'Don't come running to me,' you said, 'when you find you've bitten off more than you can chew, when you've bankrupted the place and the bailiffs are in.'"

Dinwiddie regarded the highly polished toe-caps of his boots, momentarily deflated. True, he had spoken out loudly against the idea of postal ordering, but who could have told it would do so well?

"It isn't that," he grumbled. "It's the principle of the thing, Mr David. You're forgetting my position."

"And you are forgetting *mine!*" David flung.

"Come now, gentlemen!" Luke shook an admonishing finger. "Let's not get upset! Happen you'd best leave the matter with me, Albert. David and me had best straighten it out between us, eh?"

Dinwiddie rose to his feet, well satisfied. As soon as the door closed behind him, he gloated, Luke Holroyd would put things to rights. Just a few well-chosen words from the Master would soon settle young David. And Sarah Makin would be back in the weaving-shed as fast as her rackety clogs would carry her.

He smiled a secret, malicious smile, gratified that his position had been upheld, his honour defended. A weaver from the Three-streets in his counting-house indeed! Whatever next?

"Right, lad. What've you been up to?" Luke demanded. "Can't have you upsetting Albert, can we?"

"He's an old woman, father. What's more to the point is what about *me?* Dinwiddie treats me like a boy still. He seems to forget that Low Clough will be mine, one day."

"Well now, you *do* surprise me, David. I'd never have thought you were all that concerned about the mill. Somehow I seemed to get the impression it was of no interest to you where your money came from."

"Of course I'm interested. Didn't I start up the Order-by-Post department? And isn't it doing well, in spite of all you and Dinwiddie said?"

"Aye, I'll grant you that, but there's a way of doing things. You've got to learn, son, that you can't go stepping on people's toes without a thought. Dinwiddie's a faithful servant and I get him cheap, an' all."

"I know that," the younger man conceded quietly, "but it's time I had more responsibility here."

"And by responsibility I suppose you mean that you want to do things *your* way," came the dry retort. "Want to show off your fancy schooling and spend all my brass on new-fangled ideas?"

"Low Clough is old, father. If you spend money on it now you'll be glad, later on."

"To get back to this lass," Luke changed the subject adroitly. There were two things certain to give him indigestion; parting with money and the knowledge that someone other than himself could be right. As far as he was concerned there was only one opinion at Low Clough, only one master, and that was the way it would be until Luke Holroyd JP made his peace with the Almighty.

"Well, Father?"

"Well nowt! She'll have to go back to t' shed and that's all there is to it. There's a right way and a wrong way of doing things and —"

"And the right way is *your* way, sir! You said I could run the new department yet as soon as I hire another clerk I am called into your office for a lecture!"

Luke Holroyd drew in a deep breath then let it go in a strangled snort. On the face of it, his son was right. The hiring of an extra clerk was nothing to get het up about. But the lad had stepped out of line and gone over Dinwiddie's head. He had taken on a mill-lass who clattered about and sang songs at the top of her voice. Well, he wasn't going to stand for it, nor for his son's defiance!

"Get rid of her," he ground. "Either send her back to the shed or sack her. I don't care what you do, lad, but either way I want her out of my counting-house!"

"Then you can sack her yourself, for I won't!" came the icy retort. "Or better still, tell Dinwiddie to do it. He'd enjoy that!"

The mill-master opened his mouth then closed it, speechless. His son's show of defiance should have made him angry but it hadn't. Luke was a bully, had clawed his way to the top by walking over those too weak or too afraid to stand up to him. Once he had worked at Low Clough. He had laboured, barefoot and half-naked, in the heat of the spinning-room, but with guts and guile and the luck of the devil, he had become Master. And had remained Master, an' all, and prospered too, because he'd never forgotten what it was like to be a spinner. He knew how to push a man to the ends of his endurance, when to threaten, when to give in. And now, he acknowledged warily, was a time to give in. Or to appear to. He forced a smile to his lips.

"Very well, young man. Nobody can say Luke Holroyd isn't as fair as a summer's day. I'll go to the post department and see this lass for myself. If she seems willing to learn and Josh Dobson speaks well of her, then I'll reconsider the matter."

And if he could bait her into anger, he thought cunningly, force her into a situation that showed her up in a bad light, then he would have no alternative but to sack her, would he?

There were more ways than one of skinning a

cat, Luke smiled grimly, and he knew them all!

"Well, son?" he demanded. "Are we agreed?"

Sarah knotted the string around the brown paper parcel and snipped off the ends.

"There now, Mr Dobson, that's the last of them. All packed and ready for the postman to collect," she declared triumphantly. "I think we deserve a cup of tea, don't you?"

"Then if you're making tea wi' *my* coal and in *my* time, you'd best get out an extra cup for me!"

Joshua Dobson spun round gasping to face the man whose great bulk blocked the doorway.

"Afternoon, Mr Holroyd," he whispered, his voice shaking with apprehension. "It's an honour — a *great* honour — to have you visit our Order-by-Post department."

"I see you've got yourself an assistant, Joshua." Luke raised an enquiring eyebrow. "This couldn't be the lass who was fighting like an alley-cat t'other day?"

"Aye, master, it was me." A dull flush coloured Sarah's cheeks.

"Then I hope you're not going to make a habit of it, Miss Makepiece? I hope we all in the counting-house may consider ourselves to be reasonably safe from your unladylike brawlings?"

"There'll be no bother. I only fight when I'm attacked," Sarah flung meaningfully. "And my name's *Makin*, Mr Holroyd. Caleb Makin's my father. You and him worked together in the spinning-room, if you remember."

49

"I remember, lass. Caleb got himself lamed."

"Aye, and you got yourself the mill, Mr Holroyd."

"That I did," he retorted comfortably, "and there's some who'd do well to remember that, Sarah Makin!"

Drat it, he fretted. The lass was looking at him bold as brass, challenging him with her eyes when she aught to be cringing.

"And some should try to remember what it's like to be poor," Sarah flung. "And they should bear in mind that it's not a sin to want to get on in the world!"

For a moment Joshua Dobson's timid little world trembled under the impact of two stubborn wills in close combat. Clasping and unclasping his hands he looked from one contestant to the other; from Sarah's defiantly tilted chin to Luke Holroyd's angry eyes. And then he beheld a little miracle. A small smile flickered on the mill-master's lips as he said quietly:

"So you want to get on in the world, Sarah Makin?"

"That I do!"

"By fair means or by foul, eh?"

"I reckon so, Master, though I'd rather fight clean."

The smile on Luke's lips gave way to a throaty chuckle.

"By the heck, Miss, but you've got the makings of a gradely lass, be blowed if you haven't!"

Then the laughter died and the smile faded

50

and he was the Master again, the man who ruled his little kingdom as of God-given right.

"Josh Dobson," he ground, glowering down at the man who wavered beside him. "I'm holding thee responsible for this lass's good behaviour. We'll have no more brawling and a bit less caterwauling — is that understood?"

"Oh yes, Mr Holroyd. I'll mind what you say."

"And tell her from me to get herself a pair of shoes. Them clogs of hers'll be the ruination of my floors!"

Anger sparked in Sarah's eyes. Oh, the arrogance of the man! Did he think folk fished money out of the canal? Rounding on the trembling Dobson she spat:

"And tell *him* I'd like nothing better! Ask him if he thinks I like looking as if I've just crawled out of the gutter! Tell him all I want is a chance!"

"I'm giving you a chance, Sarah Makin, but you'll do things my way, in this mill," Luke rasped. "And don't think for a minute that I've forgotten what it's like to be hungry, either. And there's summat else I'll tell you for nothing. As far as I'm concerned, there are worse tribulations in life than the wearing of clogs! Remember that, Miss, when you're on your way to the top. Remember it was Luke Holroyd told you so, an' all!" And, turning on his heel, he slammed from the room.

"Eh, Sarah," Josh breathed as the banging of a distant door confirmed that all was well again. "Eh, but that was a close shave, all right."

"Aye, Mr Dobson, I can't say I wasn't worried — for a time." Then she grinned impishly. "Happen I'd better put the kettle on! I think we deserve that cup of tea!"

The stock-pot was bubbling on the kitchen hob when Sarah reached Canal Street that evening.

"I've just put the dumplings in — won't be long," Caleb Makin smiled.

Sarah returned the greeting warily. Her father was in a rare good humour and that should have pleased her. But Caleb's small upliftings often heralded long bouts of blackest depression, and that wasn't good.

"Been busy, then?" she asked, settling herself at the fireside, wriggling her stockinged toes into the clipped cloth of the rug.

"Aye," he nodded. "Paid my last respects to Will Nuttall, heaven rest him. Sold a couple of bottles of parsley tonic, an' all. Folk always seem to get fearful for their health, after a funeral. I said as much to Robey."

"Robey Midwinter?" The name caught Sarah unawares.

"Aye. He was at the graveside."

"Why? What has Will Nuttall's burying to do with him? He doesn't even live in the Three-streets."

"He does now. But happen you'd better talk to him about it, if it bothers you, lass."

"Oh, it doesn't." Sarah shook her head airily. "I don't like that man, that's all. It's as if there's

52

trouble all around him. I just wish he'd go back to wherever he came from."

"There's no trouble around him that honest men need fear. Robey Midwinter talks good sense. Why, he sat here today and —"

"He was *here?*" Sarah demanded. "What have you and him got to talk about, Father?"

She felt a tingling of apprehension. Her father had not meant to tell her he'd had a visitor, she was certain of it. Yet the meeting seemed to have cheered him and for that she should be grateful.

"*Why*, Father?" She had to ask it.

"Oh, he had an aching tooth. I put some clove-oil in it for him."

"I see," Sarah nodded, wondering why a feeling of unease was buzzing inside her head like a trapped bee, why she couldn't be glad that for once her father appeared to have had a good day. Then she shook herself impatiently. No sense in looking for trouble. She would worry about it tomorrow, if needs be. Today she had things to do and, oh, there was such news for the telling.

"I thought," she remarked as she ladled out the steaming broth, "that I might go to Albert Court, to Maggie's. I want to have a talk with her."

"You can go, but you'll not find her in," Caleb supplied. "Maggie's going to the Mission Hall — playing the piano for the Band of Hope singing tonight. I know she'll be there. Robey's going with her."

"Why, the cheek of him!" Sarah gasped. "Is

he going to sign the pledge then, or does he fancy himself as a preacher?"

"Happen he does. Happen he doesn't," Caleb retorted flatly. "But there's some in these parts are going to have reason to remember him coming, be sure of that!"

"What do you mean? Just what is this Midwinter up to?" For he *was* up to something. *"Tell me!"*

But Caleb had said all he was prepared to say and began to eat his broth with exaggerated concentration, staring into the fire as if the answers to Sarah's probings were written in the flames.

But his eyes held a strange kind of triumph, Sarah pondered. There was the light of excitement in them as if he were waiting, breathlessly, for something to happen. And in his eyes too there were dark depths she couldn't fathom. And in that instant she was afraid, for those mocking deeps held secrets too.

❀

It was strange, Luke Holroyd mused, how much louder a clock ticked in an empty house, for this barn of a place he'd once called home *was* empty.

Tonight, as he had driven up his carriageway, there had been no thrill of elation, no pride of achievement as he regarded the house that once gave him so much pleasure. High Meadow, he'd called it in his long-ago dreams, then watched it grow, stone by stone, a tribute to his success. He had hired a gardener to bring order out of the wildness around it, then filled the rooms with good, solid furniture, the finest linen, the best silverware. When it was complete, High Meadow had been a house to be proud of, waiting for the woman he would one day bring to it as his wife.

The parlourmaid tapped gently on the door.

"Cook asks if you're ready for your dessert, sir."

"Nay, I'm not hungry.

"But it's roly-poly pudding, Mr Holroyd. Cook did it special."

He didn't doubt it. Cook always served him with homely victuals when Charlotte was away; hotpot, tripe and onions and puddings that stuck to a man's ribs. All the things, he sighed, that Charlotte regarded with amused scorn.

"I don't doubt that cook'll find somewhere to put it," he retorted dryly, reflecting on the amount of food that went begging, day after day. It was a sin to waste food, he sighed inwardly. No good ever came of it.

But no one listened to his forebodings. Why should they? They'd never known adversity. Charlotte had been born into a world warm with plenty and David thought his father's pocket was bottomless.

What would become of it all when he was gone? Luke fretted. Would David's children spend fecklessly until there was nothing left? Would Low Clough fall into the hands of money-lenders? From clogs to clogs in three generations, that's what folk said when he'd become master of Low Clough, Luke recalled grimly. He had started with nothing and that was what the third generation would end up with, they'd whispered behind his back. There were some, even yet, who would like to see him fail, he brooded, and if David didn't shape himself it would be clogs to clogs all right!

Life was very unfair. That one day he would have to leave it all behind was bad enough to contemplate; that David seemed set to marry a simpering creature and rear a generation of drones was beyond thinking about. If only, Luke grumbled silently, David would find himself a spirited lass, one who could be relied upon to fill High Meadow with lusty sons, lads with a bit of the devil in them, who could be taught to care for Low Clough. It was little enough to ask.

But it would never be, for Charlotte had other ideas. David, she asserted, had been brought up a gentleman and had to marry a lady, one who would be hand-picked by her. Already there were several lined up in the marriage-stakes, one of them linked to half the nobility in Lancashire. Charlotte's grandchildren, she vowed, would have nothing of the commonplace about their pedigrees. Give her another generation and there'd be some real thoroughbreds in the Holroyd stable!

Luke shuddered. Just to think of it made his blood run cold.

He was still brooding on the underhanded ways of Fate when his son came home.

"You're late, lad," he growled. "Supper's finished."

"I'm sorry, sir. I had some business at work that kept me."

"Oh, aye? Monkey business, was it? Now I'm warning you, David —"

"Don't worry, Father. I was quite alone. As a matter of fact, I've been going through the ledgers and what I've learned is very pleasing. The post department is doing well."

"You think so, lad?"

Luke reached for the decanter and refilled his glass. Could it be that David was beginning to care for Low Clough?

"I do, father, and it will do still better."

Mollified, Luke permitted himself a fleeting smile. If only Charlotte would stop her meddling, he yearned, their son might even yet turn into a mill-master.

"Where's Mama?" David sliced into the cheese. "I thought she'd be back."

"Well, she's not," came the flat retort. "There was a letter waiting when I got home. Your mother's decided to stay on in London for a while. It seems that the Prince of Wales is attending some charity performance at the opera and nothing would do but that your mother should be there too."

He winced afresh, just to think of the expense

of it all, for Charlotte wouldn't dream of hob-nobbing with royalty in anything less than a new gown.

But he had learned to suffer his wife's improvident ways in silence. Protests only served to drive her into a tantrum. She would storm and rage, telling him he was mean, that he didn't care for her. Then she would pack her bags in high old dudgeon and take herself off to London where she would spend more money than ever. He wondered at times what had gone wrong with their marriage, why Charlotte always seemed to get the better of him. He had been so careful in his choice of a wife. He had approached her only after the greatest deliberation. Her father was a baronet and her great-uncle, on her mother's side, had been a peer. Proudly he brought his bride to High Meadow and within a year she had given him a son. His cup of glory was full, until she slammed her bedroom door in his face, declaring her duty to be done.

"You've got your son," she shrugged. "Be content."

Selfish, Charlotte was.

Now Low Clough was his love and he had stood by and watched Charlotte rear that son in the ways of the gentry with never a thought for what was to come. Or so it had seemed, until David had come up with the idea of an Order-by-Post department. Nonsense, of course, but Luke had been so grateful for his son's sudden interest in the mill that he had gone along with the idea.

And now it was making money and David had taken on another clerk — that dark-haired lass of Caleb's. Full of fire, Luke mused; an ambitious wench. He'd enjoyed sparring with her. She was handsome too; a lass that by the looks of her would bear her children with ease. What a pity she couldn't have had a duke or two in the family instead of a morose and crippled father! But that was the way of the world. You couldn't argue with what the Almighty decreed, not even if you were Luke Holroyd JP you couldn't.

"It was good of you, sir, to give Miss Makin a chance. I appreciate it." David pulled out a chair and settled himself at the table. "Josh seems pleased with her."

"But spirited," Luke nodded cagily. "Looks as if she could be headstrong."

"Maybe," David shrugged.

"And she'll have to compose herself a bit. Can't have mill ways let loose in the counting-house. Decorum, David. Decorum."

"She'll be all right, Father, once she settles down. I'm sure she must feel different. I thought," he hazarded, glancing sideways at his father's blank face, "that I might offer to buy her a pair of shoes —"

He closed his eyes, trying to choke back the reckless slip of words, but it was too late. Already the damage had been done.

"Shoes? By the heck, I knew you were up to something!" Luke roared. "As soon as Dinwiddie told me how you'd sneaked that lass in, my nose started to twitch!"

"Sir! It's not what you think. I gave Miss Makin the job because —"

"Because you had designs on her!" the irate man supplied. "Damn it, lad, do you take me for a fool? Do you think I came to earth with the last fall of soot?"

"Father — if you'd let me —"

"I was beginning to think you were showing a bit of backbone at last, but I was wrong!" Luke thundered, refusing to be interrupted. "I'll not have carrying-on at *my* mill with one of *my* workers! I'll not have a local lass weeping and wailing all over the town that she's been wronged by a Holroyd! I don't want a work-house brat for a grandchild. Sow your wild oats if you must, David, but don't do it in Hollinsdyke. Take yourself off to t'other side of the Pennines and do your rampaging there, but —"

"Father! Be *quiet!*" David Holroyd brought down his fist with a force that set the cutlery dancing on the table-top. His face was dark with anger, his eyes flashed danger.

Luke's mouth sagged open. Never before had his son spoken so. Never, ever, had he shown such spirit. It was unbelievable. It was magnificent!

"Sir — please hear me out." The anger was gone, now, but the voice was quietly resolute. He had not intended showing his hand yet, the young man mused, but this was the time! "Yes,

I do admire Miss Makin. I think she is spirited and beautiful and I find her most desirable. But I don't wish to seduce her."

"No?" Luke gasped.

"Oh, no! When Sarah bears my sons, they'll be Holroyds, not nameless chance-children for the parish to rear. I've given the matter a great deal of thought. I intend to marry Sarah Makin if she'll have me and there's nothing that you or Mama can say will stop me! Do I make myself clear, Father?"

Three

The meeting had already started when Sarah arrived at the Mission Hall in Tinker's Row. It was so quiet that at first she thought it must have been over, but as she pushed open the door the silence was ripped wide by a sudden great cheer. Hands clapped and clogged feet stamped out a storm of approval.

"He's right! The mill-masters are evil!"

"Speak for us, Robey? Help us?"

The atmosphere in the crowded room pulsated with life and the drab walls seemed to take on a reflected glow as the man on the platform acknowledged the applause of his audience. His lips were parted in a half-smile and triumph blazed in his eyes. Robey Midwinter had wooed the men and women of the Three-streets with whispered sympathy, demanded their allegiance with words of fire, then rising up like a giant had mocked their apathy.

"Do you want to live forever on this muck-heap, work for a pittance until you drop? Isn't the labourer worthy of his hire? Did not our Lord say, 'Suffer little children to come unto me', yet you stand by and see your bairns exploited!"

The dark eyes swept the room with unhurried contempt.

"You stand like sheep, bleating silently, tipping

your caps to the mill-masters, grovelling . . ."

The words ripped into the astonished silence like bullets and each one found its mark. Women dropped weary eyes and men shuffled uneasily, unable to deny the truth of the words that wrapped them round in a lash of scorn.

"Your women grow old before their time and your children never know childhood. Your bellies are empty and will stay empty until there is such a fire in them that you can stand it no longer. And when that day comes, my brethren, you will rise as one man from the midden of your misery and speak with one voice, a mighty voice to be heard all over this land. I pray God," he whispered, "I may live long enough to see it!"

Men looked at Robey Midwinter that night and saw themselves reborn in the glow of his aura and women drank in his manliness, thrilled to the challenge in his eyes.

Could this be the Messiah, the promised one who would fight for them, uphold their dignity? Who he was, where he had come from, none cared. Sufficient that he was here, this mountain of a man, pawing the ground like a lusty buck, eager for a fight. They were with him to a man.

The cheers rose and swelled, filling the room like a battle hymn and as she stood there amid the heady tumult Sarah feared that Luke Holroyd must surely have heard the wonderful noise at faraway High Meadow. He'd hear it and come tearing down the valley with the Constabulary at his heels and the law in his pocket, eager to keep the Queen's peace and uphold the authority of every mill-master in Lancaster County.

Words were wonderful, Sarah thought bitterly. Words were cheap, like ale-house gin, and any fool could drink them in.

But Robey Midwinter's words were heady with promise. He believed, so you believed. You closed your eyes and saw a golden world where men walked with dignity and no one went hungry, a world in which it was no sin to be old or lame.

Sarah clucked with annoyance. Such things could never be. Men could talk until Judgement Day if they were so minded and it wouldn't make a ha'porth of difference to Hollinsdyke. Even God had turned his back on the place.

But imagine. Imagine green-cool woods and fields of buttercups. Imagine winding lanes and soft sunsets and snow in winter that never got dirty.

Oh, why had this man come to their town? What was there about him that brought out the worst in her? Why did she want to impress him, make him notice her? And it was all so stupid because there was no room in her life for men. She was too busy getting on in the world to be bothered with such things.

But imagine what it would be like to be Robey Midwinter's woman, to walk beside him proud as a queen, to look into his eyes and see love there, and desire.

"Come on, Sarah. Give a mite for the speaker?"

A small boy grinned up hopefully, rattling the coins in his cap.

"Here y'are, cheeky." Sarah tossed over a penny. "And keep your thieving fingers to yourself. I'm watching you!"

Watching as the man at the back of the room was watching, the man who stood unmoving in the shadows, eyes downcast yet missing nothing; the same man who only this morning had looked at her with contempt in the counting-house at Low Clough. Aaron Silk, one of Dinwiddie's clerks, taking in every word, every gesture, storing them in his maggoty little mind to tell to his betters.

By tomorrow morning Luke Holroyd would know all about Robey Midwinter.

"And what did you make of it all?" Caleb Makin demanded of his daughter as they walked home. "Didn't it fire your blood, lass?"

"I don't rightly know," Sarah hazarded, slowing her steps to match those of her father. "I got there late and didn't hear much of it. What's Robey Midwinter trying to do? Set the streets alight?"

"It'd be a blessing if he could!" Caleb flung. "I'd give what was left of my life to see Low Clough go up in smoke!"

"Aye, but Low Clough'll be standing long after you and me have gone," Sarah added dryly, "so don't take on so. It's not right of Robey to raise people's hopes. What's his business here? What is there in Hollinsdyke for the likes of him?"

"His business, my girl, is righting wrongs. He's a thorn in the flesh of the masters. He preaches against injustice."

"Talk costs nothing," Sarah spat, annoyed that even for a moment she had let her guard slip, had looked at Robey Midwinter through the eyes of a woman. "And what's more, I'm surprised at Maggie's mam for taking him in," she added, glad she had come to her sober senses again. "Just wait until Luke Holroyd hears about what's going on. Your precious Robey'll be on his way so fast his toes won't touch the cobbles and Maggie Ormerod'll be out of a job," Sarah prophesied darkly.

Men like Robey were trouble. They were tall and good to look at and their eyes held mischief. They had soft words to command and when they smiled it was fit to charm the birds from the trees. But they were *trouble.*

They said little else that evening, the man whose mind was sick as his body and the girl who had no time for love, for the meeting in the Mission Hall had touched them both.

It left Sarah more certain than ever that first impressions are often right. She had sensed unrest about Robey Midwinter, known that his easy smile masked a pitiless heart. Now, as she watched her father, she was even more sure she was right.

Crouched by the hearth, bellows huffing, Caleb

blew life into the dying fire, watching intently as the coals reddened, then blazed high. And there was a hardness in the eyes that gazed into the licking flames. It was as if he saw the blazing streets of Hollinsdyke there and in the middle of the carnage Low Clough burning in fierce retribution. But even the fire that flamed in the old man's eyes could not hide the secret triumph that smouldered there.

Sarah saw it plainly and her blood ran cold.

"Sit yourself down, Albert."

Luke Holroyd reached for a cigar. Albert Dinwiddie's face wore a confidential look and when the counting-house manager had confidences to impart, it could be a wearisome business.

Dinwiddie hitched his trouser creases delicately and settled himself. What he had heard seemed hard to believe, but Aaron Silk usually spoke the truth so it was only proper the Master be told.

Silk had a nose for goings-on. If bother threatened, he could be relied upon to sniff it out.

"There was speechifying last night at the Band of Hope meeting," Dinwiddie offered. "From what I heard, I'm afraid there's trouble afoot; Mr Holroyd."

"And who told you, Albert? Was it that ferret-faced little clerk with the fancy hair?"

He did not like Silk, but it was necessary at times to heed his tittle-tattle.

Dinwiddie sniffed, ignoring a question that needed no answer.

"There was a stranger at the Mission Hall, preaching anarchy and inciting the mob. By the heck, your ears must have been burning last night, Mr Holroyd, for he fairly had it in for you."

"Oh, aye?" Luke's right eyebrow lifted a fraction. "And who is he, this splendid apostle, and what makes him think that *my* mill is any of his business?"

"They call him Robey Midwinter. He's got lodgings in the Three-streets. A big fellow he is — handsome, so I'm told. Had the women eating out of his hand."

"And the men?"

"They were listening, sir. Stamping and shouting and agreeing with every word he said. Called you the world's worst, Midwinter did; said half the cripples in Hollinsdyke had you to thank for it. Said he'd see to it that you put guards on the machines."

"Aye? Pray continue, Albert." The voice was steely-soft.

"Said you didn't do right by your apprentices either. He reckoned as how half of 'em were nowhere near nine years old and shouldn't be working."

"Well now, isn't that strange? Since most of 'em are foundlings and without a birth certificate, I don't see how anybody could blame me for that. Were any of my workers at that meeting?"

"Aye, Mr Holroyd. Just about all of 'em. There was a collection, afterwards, and everybody gave, including Miss Sarah Makin."

"Oh, but we're living in an ungrateful world." Luke shook his head sorrowfully. "I give them work and they bite the hand that feeds them. They plead poverty yet they throw their money away like drunken sailors." He raised his eyes heavenward. "May the Lord have mercy on the undeserving poor."

"Amen to that, sir."

"Thank you for warning me, Albert. You're a good and faithful servant. I'll be mindful of your loyalty, at Christmas."

Dinwiddie rose, duty done, and minced toward the door. Poor Mr Holroyd. Ingratitude was a terrible thing, he thought, well satisfied.

At the clicking of the door-sneck, the sorrowful mask fell from the mill-master's face. His eyes narrowed into slits and his jaw shaped itself into a trap. Fury raged briefly inside him, then his expression softened into one of cunning.

There was nothing to worry about. A nod to the constable and the rabble-rousing Robey would be hustled out of town if he as much as spat on the cobbles. And as for his ungrateful, ungodly workers, as for those wretches in the Three-streets —

A smile softened the craggy face. Those wretches in the Three-streets could follow their Pied Piper to perdition if that was what they wanted. And they could toss their pennies into his hat until they starved. A fool and his money were soon parted. That was why he lived at High

Meadow and owned the mill. That was why they, the miserable fools, lived in the Three-streets, and owned nothing.

He puffed on his cigar and watched the smoke drift wraithlike to the ceiling. The settling of Master Robey could wait. At this moment there was a far more interesting matter for his attention. His son's sudden fancy for Caleb Makin's lass, for instance. Now there *was* something to chew over . . .

David Holroyd was restless. He had refused his father's invitation to luncheon then spent the past half hour gazing down into the mill-yard like a love-sick idiot. And that was exactly what he had become, he thought grimly, envying the child who seemed so close to Sarah, wishing it was he himself who sat beside her, received her smile.

"But why *her?* Why a mill-lass, when you could take your pick of half Lancashire?" his father demanded.

"I don't know, sir," he had hesitated. "I think I wanted to marry her the first time I ever saw her. This isn't a sudden decision."

He would have to take a wife, it was expected of him, but not a girl of his mother's choosing, not one of the languid young ladies who were persistently paraded at High Meadow. There had not been one of them as lovely as Sarah. Sarah was so exciting. There was a turbulence about her that roused him. He was beginning to dream

70

about her now and always in those dreams she was walking on Moor Top hill. She would smile and beckon to him, then, just as he reached out to touch her, she'd be away like a wild thing, her hair flying, bare feet skimming the grass.

"And what," his father demanded, "makes you think she'll have you? Caleb Makin's a proud old cuss and likely he's reared a proud daughter. She might laugh in your face, lad."

And that was all his father would say on the matter. He hadn't ranted or raved. He had just raised a quizzical eyebrow, then lapsed into maddening silence. And when that happened, David acknowledged uneasily, he knew to tread carefully. Luke Holroyd angry was something to beware. Luke Holroyd silent was crafty as a waggon-load of monkeys and you avoided him, if you'd the sense, as you avoided the plague.

But, desperate, David had decided that now was the time to bring things into the open.

"Ask Miss Makin to come to my office when she gets back from her dinner-break," he'd told Joshua Dobson. "Nothing to worry about," he hastened. "Just want a chat . . ."

Then he had fled from the room lest Dobson should see the flush that crimsoned his cheeks. He was acting like a lad in the bonds of calf-love, but he didn't care. He wanted Sarah for his wife and to that end he would agree to any conditions she might care to impose, anything she asked, so long as she took him. He would even marry her without love and wait, if he had to, until she came to care for him. But, by God, he would have her!

When he heard Sarah's footsteps in the passage outside, David took a deep gulp of air, then settled himself uneasily behind his desk.

"Josh said you wanted me?"

She smiled and closed the door behind her.

"Yes, Miss Makin." Jumping to his feet, he offered a chair, taking her elbow, handing her into it. The feel of her warm, bare skin sent need flaming through him and he allowed his hand to remain on hers.

"Is something wrong, Mr David?"

He felt her body stiffen as she pulled away her arm, her eyes instantly guarded. Her withdrawal was intended and obvious. It acted as a sharp, silent reprimand, a sobering reminder that she was not for touching.

"No, Sarah. Nothing's wrong." He sat down heavily again, damning his stupidity.

The eyes that levelled with his sparked defiance, demanding he keep his right and proper place. He read the message clearly. He was a Holroyd and she a spinner's daughter. The gulf between them was wide and deep, so think on!

"I wanted to ask you," he floundered, latching on to the first thought that drifted into his muddled mind, "about the Band of Hope meeting last night."

Sarah's chin shot out and up, her eyes narrowing.

"What makes you think I can tell you anything about it?"

"Because you were there, Sarah, and I hoped you'd tell me what happened."

"I got to the meeting late, so I don't rightly know what went on. But why don't you ask Aaron Silk?" she flung, her lips tight with distaste.

David Holroyd's head jerked upward. "I know nothing about Silk," he rapped. "My father told me about the meeting, then asked me to get to the truth of it."

Liar! His father had asked no such thing. His father had told him about the meeting then laughed defiance. Let them listen to Midwinter until their clog-irons rusted! he'd said. Empty heads made empty bellies. If that was what his workers wanted, they were perfectly free to choose.

"Tell me, Sarah — who is this man Midwinter? I heard he has lodgings in the Three-streets."

"Happen he has, but it's of no interest to me. And as to who he is," she shrugged. "Then your guess is as good as mine."

Sarah wriggled uneasily. She didn't like being questioned or having to meet and return David Holroyd's stare.

"Then I'd guess he's nothing but a rabble-rouser," he flung, "who thinks he can teach my father his business. Don't the workers at Low Clough know that if they've got a grievance they have only to see Mr Luke?"

73

"You mean nobody's ever told the Master about the bad lighting in the spinning-mill and the cold in the weaving-shed?" Sarah mocked. "He'd put it to rights, would he, if he knew? And fix guards on the machines and free the apprentices?"

"*Free* them? You talk as if they were caged! We give them work, pay them a wage —"

"Which goes straightway to the ale-house or is grabbed by the workhouse-master to help pay for his charity. Either way, those bairns are losers!"

"You feel strongly about the children, don't you, Sarah?" Here could be a way to her heart. "Tell me what I can do to help."

"I don't rightly know," she shrugged, caught off guard by the abruptness of such an offer.

"Then put yourself in my place. If you could, how would *you* help the orphans?"

"I'd feed them, poor little souls." Her eyes were gentle again. "They're always hungry. They work nearly seven hours in the mill then go straight to school. Their insides must ache with emptiness."

"Is that why you give food to the child, every day in the yard?"

"Billy-Boy? Yes," she smiled. "I share what I have with him but it's only a drop of charity in a sea of want. Bairns should be fed regular. It's their need and their right. Either that, or people shouldn't bring them into the world!"

"But Sarah — having children is Nature's way of things. Children are a fact of life."

"Then more's the pity. A child should be wanted, not a burden. Aye, sir," she flung. "That's what most bairns are in the Three-streets. *Burdens!*"

The animation had left her face and in its place was a yearning sadness. David saw that look and knew there was hope.

"Sarah," he said gently. "I want to help. I know how much needs to be done, but Low Clough isn't mine yet, and I must make haste slowly."

"You truly care, Mr David? Enough to want to do something about it?"

He nodded silently, amazement bursting inside him, realising that whatever Sarah wanted he wanted too. It was merely that the thought had never crossed his mind before. And until now, if he dared to be honest, he hadn't much cared either. But to love Sarah was to look at the world through her eyes.

The hooter blared and Sarah jumped instinctively to her feet.

"I must go, but — but if you really care, Mr David, couldn't you put it to the Master? A bowl of broth costs next to nothing, but it would mean a lot to a hungry child."

"Sarah!"

Her hand was on the door latch. Any moment she'd be gone and a chance lost. He had to ask her! *Now!*

"Wait, Sarah. There's something else!"

"Yes?"

"Marry me, Sarah? Say you'll marry me and

I'll do anything — anything at all you ask!"

The words sounded strange, as if other lips had formed them. What had he done? He waited, his heart pounding.

Sarah turned slowly, her eyes wide with disbelief, and then, as if her legs were suddenly useless, she leaned heavily against the door.

"Did you say *marry* you, Mr David? Have you taken leave of your senses?" Her words came in a whisper of anger. "Or is it a game, a joke?"

"No! I mean it. I love you."

"Love me? You don't even *know* me! A week ago we hadn't even met!"

"That isn't true," he urged. "I've known you much longer than that, but you didn't realise it. All last summer, when you walked on Moor Top, I was there watching you. I'd go almost every night, hoping to see you, wanting to speak to you, wondering who you were . . ."

"Then you'd only to ask," she retorted bitingly, "and I'd have told you!"

"I realise that now," he admitted. "But I was afraid if I approached you you'd run away."

"I'd have told you," she continued doggedly, "that I was Sarah Makin, that I lived in Canal Street, that my mam was dead and my father only half alive, that —"

"I know all that," he interrupted softly.

"And?"

"I only know I love you and want to marry you. Nothing else matters."

"Oh, Lordy," she breathed. "What a mess!"

"A mess, Sarah? Would it be so very terrible to be married to me?" he gasped. "Wouldn't you like a fine home, a carriage of your own, all the dresses you could dream of, pairs and pairs of shoes?"

"Of course I would," she whispered, wide-eyed. "But to take all that without having anything to give in return wouldn't be decent."

"Give me yourself. That's all I ask."

"No, Mr David. It wouldn't be right. Oh, I reckon I could be a wife to you, but I'd be cheating, for all that and it would be wrong. Even a mill-girl has her pride."

"I don't understand you, Sarah. What has marriage to do with pride?"

"It means that if I took all you offered I'd be sinking to the level of the gutter," she whispered, her eyes downcast. "I'd be selling myself, wouldn't I, because there'd be no love in it — not for me, anyway."

"But many a young lady marries without love, then comes to care for her husband."

"It wouldn't work." Solemnly Sarah shook her head. "And even if I loved you there'd be your parents to think about."

Oh, think of it, she fretted. Think what the proud Mrs Holroyd would say to a mill-girl for a daughter. And think about the rumpus there'd be an' all in the Three-streets. They'd say Sarah Makin had gone off her head and they'd laugh themselves silly. Then, when the laughing was over, they'd turn their backs on her because she wouldn't be one of them any more. They'd hate her more than they hated the mill-masters because she'd be a turncoat.

But, oh, imagine living in a house as grand as High Meadow. Imagine riding in a carriage, having shoes of softest leather and little pink slippers. And lazing each morning in a soft, warm bed; her *husband's* bed.

"I'm sorry," she heard herself say. "I'm mindful of the honour you do me, but I can't marry you, *sir.*"

She laid great stress on the last word, so it should emphasise the divide between them, but he chose to ignore it.

"I won't give up, Sarah. I shall ask you again. I'll ask until you say yes."

Lost for words, bewildered and dismayed, Sarah fled.

"What is it, lass?" Josh asked. "What's upset you? Mr David's not found fault with your work?"

"No, Mr Dobson. Nothing like that. Nothing to worry about," she whispered, forcing her lips into a smile.

Nothing at all to worry about except that somehow she had landed herself feet first in trouble again. Oh, Lordy. Why did it always have to happen to Sarah Makin?

Dismissing a problem, Sarah discovered, did not guarantee that it would go away. She had firmly decided to forget what had taken place, disturbing though it had been. She would forget it as if it had never happened.

But it had not been as easy as that and the vexed question was still there, niggling inside her head as she lay wide-eyed in her bed, counting the quarters that chimed from a distant clock.

Why had Mr David spoiled things? She had been so happy about her promotion. Joshua Dobson was a kindly soul and there were no overlookers to watch her, no machine noise crashing inside her head, no fines. Just to think about buying her first pair of shoes had stood out like a milestone in her life, yet now she was being promised pairs and pairs of them.

She wished she could have shared her problem with her father, but mill-masters in general and Luke Holroyd in particular brought out the worst in him. Caleb Makin was the last person she could confide in.

But share her worry she had to and it had to be Maggie she would tell. And even if her friend could not help, she reflected, a trouble shared would be a trouble halved. Nor would Maggie shout her confidences all over Hollinsdyke, for being proposed to by a mill-owner's son wasn't a thing to be bandied about. For the most part, mill-owner's sons were slippery customers and a working girl remembered that if she didn't want to end up in trouble.

Without a doubt, her secret would be safe with Maggie, but wasn't it a pity Robey couldn't know about it? Not that he mattered, of course! But to have seen the amazement on his face would have been nothing short of wonderful. And when he had recovered from the shock he'd be glad she had said no, look at her in a new light, show her a bit more respect, like as not.

And that was a puzzle, if you like, because she didn't like the man at all and it didn't matter one bit what he thought of her.

Sarah sighed and pulled the blanket over her head. There would be time for a chat before she went to work. Maggie would know what was best to be done. Maggie would straighten things out for her.

There was a softness about the early morning that made Sarah look up to the distant hills. High on Moor Top there would be birdsong and fat little leaf-buds ready to burst. And the spiky blackthorn that grew beside the beck would be a froth of white blossom.

Undaunted, she swung into Albert Court and stopped at the third house down. She felt almost happy. Strange, this churning inside her. She shouldn't, she supposed, be feeling so light of heart and there shouldn't be a kind of breath-lessness inside her, as if she were a child again and this were Christmas Eve. It wasn't, it really wasn't anything to do with Robey Midwinter. The giddy feeling was nothing to do with his being there. Robey was a rabble-rouser. He had a tongue that could wound and eyes that mocked. His sort were best left alone and she knew it. Then why, she thought irritably, was she getting herself into such a state?

She didn't tap on the back door or even call out. There was no need. No 3, Albert Court was open house to Sarah Makin.

At first everything seemed so still she was sure the kitchen was empty, then in the dimness she caught a movement, heard the whispering of a sigh.

Robey stood there and, in his arms, Maggie. They did not hear the opening of the door or Sarah's gasp of alarm. They were kissing. Their embrace was long and passionate, their bodies touched. Robey, his arms cradling Maggie's waist; Maggie, pink and pretty, her hair disarranged, so small beside him that she reached on tiptoe to meet his lips.

Sarah backed out of the room, cold with shock, stunned and disbelieving.

No! Not Maggie and Robey? Maggie wasn't his kind. She was too gentle, too trusting. And she had no right to him when Sarah Makin wanted him. Oh, it was useless to deny it. In that small moment of realisation she had wanted to sink her nails into Maggie's face and draw blood; had felt a sickening urge to tangle her fingers in the pale yellow hair and, screaming, pull her from his arms.

Rage danced before Sarah's eyes. She picked up her skirts and ran blindly.

She was late arriving at the mill for she had walked aimlessly, unthinking and uncaring. The shock of her anger had lessened but the agony of her friend's betrayal had not.

But see if Sarah Makin cared! Let them have their stolen kisses, if that was what they wanted; it was nothing to her. Only let them wait, and she would show them!

She clattered up the staircase and along the counting-house passage. Outside David Holroyd's office she stopped, tossed back her head, then knocked loudly on his door.

"Sarah!" He rose quickly to his feet. "My dear, what is wrong?" Gently his finger touched the tear that lay on her cheek. "You've been crying!"

"No! I was late, that's all. I was running . . ."

She drew in a shuddering breath, then dropping her eyes to her hands she said slowly:

"I came here to say something. I'd be grateful if you could spare me a minute, Mr David. I'd like to get it over with."

For just a moment it seemed she could not go on, then straightening her shoulders, staring at the wall above his head, she whispered,

"Yesterday, sir, you asked me to marry you and I said I couldn't. I'd like to change my mind. I'm saying yes."

"Sarah!" He stared at her bemused. "I can't believe it. You turn me down, then out of the blue you say —"

"I see. You've thought better of it," she demanded harshly. "It was a joke. You don't want me?"

"Of course I want you, but—"

"But you don't want to *marry* me?" she supplied. "I'm a mill-girl and gentlemen don't marry the likes of me. They only —"

"Sarah! Sit down, and shut up — *please!* Of course I want to marry you. It came as a shock, that's all. Yesterday I cursed my stupidity for flinging it at you so clumsily. I thought I had lost you. Now, you've turned completely about face. Why, Sarah?"

"I don't know," she shrugged. "Happen I've had time to think about it." What was she about? Cutting off her nose to spite her face, that's what! And it was Robey Midwinter's fault; his and Maggie's! "Happen I've come to realise the honour you do me —"

"Honour? Oh, my dear," he said gently, "that's a silly word!" Then he shrugged and smiled and taking her hands in his own said softly, "It doesn't really matter what your reasons are. Just so long as you'll marry me that is all I want to hear you say."

"I'll marry you, Mr David," she whispered. "And I *will* try. If you'll put up with my ways, teach me how a lady should act —"

"No. You mustn't change. All you must learn is how to love me. Oh, you've been honest with me," he hastened, silencing the protest that sprang to her lips. "But you will come to love me, Sarah. And I shall never give you cause for regret."

She didn't speak. She couldn't. There was a great pain inside her and tears in a tight knot in her throat. She tried to smile, but her lips were stiff with misery.

"We'll be married at once, my love. I'll see the Bishop, get a licence to have the banns waived. I won't give you time to change your mind." He squeezed her hands gently, realising for the first time how cold they were, how they trembled. "You'll not change your mind, Sarah?"

She shook her head, her eyes downcast. *Never have cause for regret?* But already she was filled with remorse. She had been stupid again, blundering in without thought. Blinded by jealousy and anger she had excelled herself this time. Already she regretted her rashness, and serve her right too. Only Sarah Makin could be so foolish, promise herself in marriage to one man whilst every small part of her cried out for another.

Oh, damn Robey Midwinter! Maggie was welcome to him! Let her wed him and see if Sarah Makin cared! And she wasn't weeping, she really wasn't.

Then like a frightened child she went blindly into David's waiting arms and sobbed as if her heart was ready to break.

Four

Sarah walked moodily, kicking the grass with a petulant toe, trying to ignore the feeling of panic that surged inside her each time she allowed herself to think about the day to come.

The air was warm with the scent of awakening earth and tender growing things and here, on Moor Top hill, Hollinsdyke seemed far away. But for the drift of church-bells ringing out below her, she could have imagined herself into another world.

She willed the bells to stop. They reminded her uneasily about tomorrow, the day she was trying hard to forget.

She hadn't told a soul yet; not even her father. How would he react, she fretted, when she said:

"I'm going to be married, Father. Tomorrow I shall wed Luke Holroyd's son."

He would be bitterly angry and it would take him a long time to get used to the idea.

Why was everything in such a turmoil? Why had Mr David rushed things so? Had he thought she would call it off with the first reading of the banns? Had he really believed that to be married quickly by special licence would save her from three weeks of wagging tongues and sly nods?

It wasn't the talk she was worried about. More than gossip she feared her father's fury, for sometimes she thought it was only his hatred of Luke Holroyd that kept him alive.

'One day,' he had said, 'Luke Holroyd's going to get his comeuppance and I want to live long enough to see it. I want to stand there, and laugh.'

"We'll make it a quiet wedding, if that's what you want," David had said and nowhere, Sarah acknowledged, was quieter than the parish church at nine on a Monday morning. There was almost an air of furtiveness about it.

But at least it would not be raining tomorrow, she thought gratefully, looking up at the rosy evening sky. She wouldn't feel so badly about it, if the sun shone.

David had said she had to have a wedding-dress.

"Buy something blue," he said, offering her a handful of sovereigns.

"When we're wed, Mr David, you can buy my clothes," she retorted, more sharply than she had intended, "but until then you'll take me as I am, or not at all!"

It had been a deliberate act of defiance. Had he protested, she could have walked out of his life. But he was careful not to give her the chance.

"I'm sorry, my darling. I'll not care what you wear — only come?" He had smiled then and chided her gently. "And when we are married you must learn to call me David. I shall put you across my knee and spank you if you call me mister!"

He had said it kindly, yet Sarah bristled with indignation. Spank her indeed? Only let him try, and he'd feel her clog-irons against his shins! But it mattered little, she shrugged, for David Holroyd's like didn't do such things. With Robey Midwinter, now, it would be a different matter. Robey wouldn't take nonsense from any woman. To be spanked by him would be an altogether different experience and to kiss and make up afterwards would be nothing short of wonderful.

But Robey didn't love her. Angry for letting herself think about him again she tried to force him out of her mind. That he belonged to Maggie was beyond doubt. When a man and woman kiss as they had kissed, marriage must surely follow.

Yet it isn't easy to dismiss a man when suddenly he is there, not a hundred yards away, walking the hillside with great swinging strides.

Sarah gasped, not wanting to believe it, her heart pounding with happiness because it was undeniably true. Scrambling to her feet she took a deep, calming breath.

"Good-evening, Mr Midwinter," she called, marvelling at her primness, glad he could not see the tightly-clenched fists thrust deep into her pockets.

"How-do, Sarah Makin? Come up here after some fresh air, have you?"

"Aye," she nodded.

"My, but it's good to get away from the muck." He threw himself to the ground then patted the grass at his side. "Sit down, lass, and talk to me."

The familiar arrogance was gone and as she looked into his eyes Sarah saw they were without scorn.

"What about?" Cautiously she dropped to her knees beside him. "Want to ask questions again?"

"Not today," he smiled. "I know all I need to know about Hollinsdyke, for the time being."

He settled his hands behind his head and shut his eyes as if to announce the subject was closed.

Sarah shifted uneasily. She wasn't at all sure how this different Robey should be handled.

"How is your tooth?" she ventured, trying to keep her voice even. "Father said you'd had a bad ache."

"*Me?*" He opened his eyes and laughed up at her. "Sure you're not mistaking me for someone else?"

"N-no. Father said he'd put oil of cloves in it."

Instantly the suspicions she had felt took substance. Her father had acted strangely, as if he had not intended telling her that Robey had been to the house. Now it was obvious he'd had a reason for lying.

"I called on your father, but not with an aching tooth," Robey admitted easily, closing his eyes again.

Oh, but he was handsome. Sarah acknowledged. Just to look at him sent small sinful shivers tingling through her. She wanted to touch him, trail her finger across the outline of his face, brush his lips with her own. What would it be like, she wondered, to feel his arms around her?

"What are you thinking about, Sarah Makin?"

His voice crashed into her secret thoughts and she flushed, angry he had caught her looking at him so intently.

"I was wondering who you are," she lied, "and why you are here."

"You were at the meeting," he shrugged. "You should know what I'm here to do."

"But it won't be any use!" she protested. "You'll never change things. Men have tackled Luke Holroyd before, and come to grief."

"I can try," he retorted amiably. "At least I can say I cared."

"And I care too," Sarah cried. "I care about the children, anyway."

"And your father — crippled by wilful neglect? Doesn't he matter?"

"Of course he matters," Sarah flung, trying not to be goaded into anger. "But he had a choice, and the children haven't. My father could have walked out of Low Clough any time he'd a mind to. But the bairns are different. They're little and weak and they don't have a choice. They can't fight back. Bother about *them!*"

For a moment he didn't speak, leaving Sarah to fume inwardly that he had succeeded in upsetting her yet again. Then slowly he said:

"So you do care? There *is* something other than self inside that head of yours?" He reached over and took her hand in his. "I'm glad, Sarah. I'm glad."

She closed her eyes helplessly, for the sudden delight of his approval was almost more than she could bear. She felt the pressure of his hand, his cheek close to her own. Tilting her head, breathless with joy, she parted her lips to receive his kiss.

But he did not kiss her. He laughed instead and pulled her to her feet.

"Come on, lass. I'll walk you home. I promised Maggie's mother I'd not be late for supper."

With a gasp of dismay Sarah's eyes flew open. His words were like cold water thrown carelessly into her face and they had the same shocking effect. Trying to collect her reeling senses she stood bemused as he turned his back on her and strode towards the path that led down to the town.

Damn the man! Damn him for making her care! But he was in for a shock, she fumed. She would show him how little he meant to her! Tomorrow she was marrying David Holroyd and Robey Midwinter could go to the devil, for all she cared!

"Wait for me," she called, loving him so much it was like a fire raging inside her.

He stopped and held out his hand and she placed her own inside it, thrilling as an exquisite pain shot through her.

They walked without speaking and then, where the path crossed the beck on large, flat stones, he stopped, dropping to his knees at the foot of the blackthorn.

"Look, Sarah — primroses. Now there's a sign that summer's a-coming."

Gently he gathered the pale little blossoms, then, binding them together with a wisp of dried grass, solemnly gave them to her.

"Flowers for my lady," he smiled.

Pain stabbed at Sarah's heart. Didn't he know what he was doing to her? She wanted to crush the flowers, fling them away, but she cupped them tenderly in her hands, for they were the most precious things she had ever beheld. She knew she should thank him, smile into his eyes as if the giving and receiving of flowers was a commonplace thing, but she could not. A smile comes hard to a woman's lips when her heart is weeping.

'Let tomorrow come quickly,' she prayed, 'and let it pass quickly too. You see, Lord, I'm cutting off my nose to spite my face. I love Robey and I can't have him and it's all such a mess . . .'

And then, as if her prayer had been heard, Sarah knew where the answer lay.

She would tell her father about it, just as she had intended telling Maggie. She would ask his advice and she would act on it too. Marriage was a serious thing and her father was older and wiser by far than she. Caleb Makin would know what was to be done.

Decision taken, she smiled into Robey's eyes. It was as if a great unhappiness had been banished, as though in a twinkling she were free of her own foolishness, for she knew exactly the advice her father would give.

Caleb Makin was sitting by the fireside, staring fixedly into the flames when Sarah got home. He didn't move as she entered and she knew that the previous day's elation had turned, as it always did, into black depression.

"See, Father," she coaxed. "Primroses from Moor Top."

Slowly Caleb raised his eyes, his face blank and bitter. His shoulders lifted in a small shrug and Sarah knew that this was not the time to tell him her secret or ask his advice. It was as if he had pulled a curtain of resentment around himself and there was no way through it.

She knew there would be no help for her now. She could talk to her father all night and he would not hear a word she uttered. He would just sit there, in his little private hell.

"And I," she thought, "will marry David Holroyd as I said I would, because there's no getting out of it."

She filled a cup with water, then tenderly placed the flowers in it.

"They were growing by the beck," she whispered to the uncaring room. "Pretty little things, aren't they?"

Flowers Robey had picked for her. Flowers from her love.

Sarah awoke long before Limping Ned knocked

on the windows of Canal Street. Reluctantly she stretched and sat up in bed, looking round the little room, knowing she was doing it for the last time.

Where would she sleep tonight? They hadn't talked about it, she and David, but there had been so little time. Five days ago he had asked her to marry him yet only last week she had been looking forward to her first day in the counting-house.

It was her own fault they had not talked. She had been deliberately vague, shutting it out of her mind as if to ignore it was to postpone its coming.

But this was the day on which she was to marry a mill-master's son. This drab, half-awake still-ness was her wedding-morning and a small breath of fear caught in her throat. Then realising there was nothing to be gained in delay, she wrapped her shawl around her shoulders and slipped silently downstairs.

She was surprised to see the kitchen fire blazing and the kettle puffing steam on the hob. Usually her father lay abed until the clatter of clogs out-side proclaimed a new day. But today he too seemed restless.

"Good-day, lass. You're up early."

"I couldn't sleep."

Her father seemed better. Now, thanks be, she could tell him. Soon she would have to be at the church. The matter had been put off for long enough.

"Tea?" Caleb asked.

"Please. And Father — come and sit by the fire. There's something I want to tell you."

"Bad news, is it?"

"No." Her father always expected the worst, but he couldn't be blamed for that. "It's just that I'm getting married —"

The old man looked up sharply, his eyes questioning.

"Well?" Sarah demanded. "Aren't you going to say anything?"

"What is there to say?" Caleb's eyes narrowed. "You didn't even think to mention you were walking out, so why should it matter all that much when suddenly you tell me you're thinking of getting wed?"

"Not thinking, Father. It's decided. It's this morning, at nine o'clock."

Caleb set down his mug, splashing tea on the hearthstone.

"I see," he jerked. "Since you've waited this long to tell me, I can only reckon you've got yourself into trouble."

"If you mean am I going to have a baby," Sarah cried, "then I'm not. Certain sure I'm not! I didn't tell you because I knew you'd be upset."

"Upset?" he ground. "Why should I be upset? Doesn't every lass get wed, sooner or later? But I thought you had more sense, Sarah Makin. I thought you were going to get on in the world."

"Then happen I just might be," she whispered, tears pricking her eyes. "Only it's a sad day when I can't ask my own father to give me away."

"And why not? If you've got your heart set on it, then I'll come with you to the chapel, lass."

"Will you?" she choked, her voice a whisper of torment. "When I tell you I'm marrying David Holroyd, will you come, Father?"

For a moment the silence in the little room was so complete that Sarah could feel it screaming a warning. Then, with a terrible cry, Caleb lifted his hand and brought it crashing into his daughter's face.

"Trollop!" he hissed. "I see it all, now! Setting you to work in the counting-house, giving you ideas above your station. *My* lass, marrying a Holroyd! I never thought I'd see the day," he spat, his eyes burning hate, "when I'd take my hand to my own girl. But as from this day, Miss, you're no longer mine. I'm going out, for the sight of you sickens me. Go to your fine lover! Go anywhere, only don't be here when I come back! Don't *ever* come to this house again, my fine lady. You'll not be welcome!"

With a cry that was almost a sob, he dashed his hand across his eyes and snatching up his jacket slammed out of the house.

Sarah stood still as a statue, listening shocked to the dragging of his foot on the cobbles outside until she could hear it no longer.

Tears rose in her throat in a great choking lump and she bit hard on her fist to prevent herself from giving way.

Why had her father done this to her? He had only needed to forbid the marriage and she would have obeyed him. Gladly she would have obeyed him.

But she wouldn't weep, not on her wedding-day. It was unlucky, wasn't it, and she had had all the bad luck she was prepared to take.

Why had her father made it necessary for them to part in anger? But perhaps, she sighed, when he came to realise he could not keep himself without her help, he might make her welcome again.

Would he though? Caleb Makin would beg for parish relief, end up in the workhouse even, rather than take Holroyd money. And from this day on, she conceded, it would be Holroyd money she would be offering him.

Suddenly she could stand it no longer. She wanted to be as far away from the Three-streets as she could get. She wanted to be away from her father's house, no matter what her future held. And she would marry David Holroyd, and be damned to them all! What lay ahead she could only wonder about and fear, a little, but there was nothing she could do now to change things. She had given her word and she would keep it. She had made her bed, hadn't she? Well now she would lie on it!

Rounding the corner into Church Street, Sarah stopped short. Now, if she was to do it, was the moment to call a halt, the time to say no. Even yet, it was all slightly unreal. It was as if she had stepped, unthinking, on to a roundabout, a gaudy prance of wooden horses, rotating so quickly that it was impossible to get off and run back to the dreary safety of the Three-streets.

But she had passed the point of no return when quietly she closed the door behind her and, crying inside herself, walked away without so much as a backward glance.

Now, grouped around the church gate like an unreal tableau, was her future, David Holroyd standing erect, his morning-coat immaculate, his top-hat set at a stiff, anxious angle. And by his side the verger fidgeted, looking at his pocket-watch, wishing, she shouldn't wonder, he had not been called upon to witness this hole-and-corner wedding.

Only the coachman seemed at ease as he waited beside Luke Holroyd's best carriage, soothing the restive horses.

David looked up and saw her standing there.

"Sarah!" he called, running to meet her, taking her hand in his lest even now she should turn and flee. "Dearest, you've come."

"Of course I've come," she choked. "I said I would, didn't I?"

"I know," he smiled. "But I was anxious." He entwined his fingers in hers then tucked her arm beneath his own.

"Nervous, Sarah? I know I am."

"Me too," she nodded. "But it isn't too late,

Mr David. If you've thought better of it, now's the time to say so."

"Oh, no," he jerked. "There's no getting rid of me now." Then his forehead wrinkled into a frown. "Your father isn't coming?"

"No," she whispered, colouring deeply. "He had one of his turns. Does he have to be here?"

Maybe they couldn't be wed if there wasn't someone to give her away, she thought wildly. She didn't understand church ways. She had been Band of Hope all her life. Maybe, without her father, the wedding couldn't take place?

"No, Sarah. It needs just you and me and two witnesses — and the vicar, of course."

"All right, then," she said, tilting her chin. "Happen we'd better go."

The church clock began to strike nine. It was too late now for regrets. For better or worse, Sarah conceded, this was her wedding-day, and nothing would ever be quite the same again.

Their steps echoed loudly in the empty church. Before them on the chancel steps stood the vicar, his book open at the ready. He nodded a reluctant greeting, then, nervously clearing his throat, began to speak the words of the marriage service.

"Dearly beloved. We are gathered together here in the sight of God and in the face of this congregation — in the er — presence of these witnesses . . ."

What a mess he was making of it! But it was

upsetting, a Holroyd getting married in such a way. Nor did the vicar care for special licence affairs. He wondered uneasily if Mr Holroyd knew about this morning's goings-on and he didn't dare even begin to imagine Mrs Holroyd's thoughts on the matter. But there was nothing he could do; he sighed and, squaring his shoulders, resumed the chant.

". . . to join together this Man and this Woman —"

The verger stood rigid, staring ahead at the sombre purple of the altar-cloth, wondering why they couldn't have waited until Easter to get themselves tied. Didn't they know Lent weddings were unlucky, the silly young things?

The scrubbing-woman who was cleaning the church porch when the vicar asked her to stand witness wiped a tear from her eye and smiled gently. She loved a wedding, even a wedding like this one without kith or kin or well-wisher present. She hoped the bride would have no regrets. Such a bonny, sad-eyed lass . . .

David Holroyd looked with love at the woman who stood beside him.

With this ring, I thee wed and with all my worldly goods I thee endow.

All he had he would gladly give her. Soon he would be able to buy her everything she could want. Soon. When she was his.

Those whom God hath joined together, let no man put asunder.

The vicar's voice droned into his thoughts. It

was almost over. She was his wife now. Dear, wide-eyed Sarah whose face was pale and whose hand trembled in his. Sarah in a drab grey skirt and cheap white blouse with a bunch of primroses pinned bravely to her shawl. Dear God, how he would cherish her!

❦

"Happy, Sarah?"

"Happy?" she echoed, gazing around her at the breathtaking litter of boxes and parcels. "Why, yes — yes, I am . . ."

But it couldn't be happiness, this churning inside her. Bewilderment, excitement, agitation like as not. But happiness — no.

Since the church clock struck nine she had been in a half-dream, unwilling to awaken to face up to this fateful day. She had become an ostrich, she thought. All fine feathers and head in the sand.

Vaguely she remembered the church, cold and musty-smelling, the vows she had made, David's kiss. Out of the shadows came fleeting recollections of the drive to the railway station, the journey to Manchester and the shock of her first real encounter with David's world.

"Now I shall take you shopping," he smiled.

They had stopped at the store to buy the dress he was so set upon and ended up by buying the entire place, or so it seemed to Sarah.

The gown David chose was of silk, the colour of the first forget-me-not, its skirt pulled back into the newly-fashionable bustle, its cuffs and neckline edged with matching lace.

Bemused, she fondled its rustling folds. It was the most beautiful dress she had ever seen; just to touch it made her want to weep.

But her husband's generosity had not stopped at the purchase of a single gown. They bought house dresses and street dresses, petticoats, ribbon-threaded under-pinnings, bonnets and gloves. And cotton stockings and silk stockings, button-boots, shoes, slippers trimmed with swansdown.

"Please — no more," Sarah begged, guilt thrashing inside her. It was downright sinful. They had spent so much she had lost count. Pounds and pounds. More than the whole of the Three-streets could earn in a month.

He was trying so hard, she thought miserably, willing herself to respond to his kindness, wishing she could shake herself out of the dream.

"I love you so much," he whispered. "Please, my darling, don't look so sad. Everything will be all right. I promise."

"I know," she choked, "and I'm grateful. Truly I am."

But gratitude was the last thing he wanted of this woman who was now his wife. He wanted her love, wanted her to say the words he so longed to hear.

But one day she would say them, he vowed. He would make her so happy she wouldn't be able to help herself. Only let it be soon, he yearned. Let it be soon.

Sarah hung the last of the gowns in the massive mahogany wardrobe then closed the drawer on the dainty undergarments. Soon she would awaken. Soon she would open her eyes and find she was sitting by the hearth at Canal Street, wondering about the dream she had just had.

"What am I to do with these?" she hesitated.

Only one box remained unpacked. In it were her mill clothes. They looked almost comic, laid carefully between crisp tissue paper, folded as painstakingly as the most luxurious of her dresses.

"Will Madam be needing *these?*" the shop assistant had asked, holding the skirt and shawl between a disdainful finger and thumb. Sarah was about to ask her to throw them away, but David had told the girl to pack them in a box, if she pleased, and have them delivered with the rest.

"Why did you want to keep them? The lady in the shop looked at them as if they'd bite her. They're poor things, worth nothing."

"You wore them to our wedding. I want them to be kept," he said firmly.

"Why?" she insisted. "I'd have thought you'd not want reminding of what I was, where I came from. I thought you'd be ashamed . . ."

"Then you thought wrongly, my Sarah."

She shrugged, not understanding. But if that was what he wanted then so be it. It was fair exchange for all he had given her.

They dined later in the privacy of their room. It was surely the most magnificent room in the world, she decided. Ainderby must be exactly like this, she marvelled as they were bowed through the glittering glass doors of the Manchester hotel. There had been potted palms and greenery everywhere and gilt chairs, plush-covered, and the grandest staircase she had ever seen, smothered in thick red carpet.

Their rooms were even more opulent, but after the first shock had passed the richness faded and became one more part of the unreality.

Sarah wore the blue silk and coping with the bustle would have been a near disaster if David had not had the sense to ring for a maid to help her into the dress.

Shyly she watched as a small army of servants set a table with silver and glass and little posies of pale pink rosebuds. Waiters followed to serve their meal, then coughing discreetly had left them alone in the flickering candlelight.

Sarah ate little but drank the wine because it was cool and the champagne because of the novelty of it. But for the most part she sat with hands clenched, tension coiled inside her like an overwound spring, her head growing lighter, her eyes growing heavier.

She looked again at the gold ring that made her hand feel odd, proof beyond doubt that she must surely have been married. She still walked in the mists of make-believe but the ring could not be ignored. It was very solid and very real.

The candles burned lower and a chambermaid tapped on the door, asking to be allowed to turn down the bed.

"Sweetheart," David smiled when they were alone again. "Don't be afraid?"

"I'm not afraid — not really," she whispered, "but it's like a dream, Mr David, and it's happened so sudden-like that I can't seem to catch up with it."

She glanced through the open door of the bedroom. The pink-shaded lamps had been lit, the satin bedcover removed. Folded neatly on one pillow lay her husband's nightshirt and draped mockingly across the other was the new white nightdress. It was decorously styled with long, full sleeves and a high neckline demurely frilled, but it was so flimsy, so blatantly transparent that she blushed just to look at it.

One by one, the candles flickered and died and the mantel clock chimed midnight. David pushed back his chair and rose to his feet.

"Sarah?" he said gently, holding out his hand.

The room tilted slightly, then righted itself and she walked with him to the bedroom.

By the dressing-table she paused. Lying forlorn beside the silver-backed brushes was the little bunch of primroses, fresh still, as though they had just been gathered.

Without another thought she took them, then, shuddering at the wickedness of it, tossed them into the glowing coals.

"Sarah!" David cried. "Your wedding flowers!"

She watched unspeaking as they shrivelled, burned briefly, then were gone. Only then did she say:

"It doesn't matter. They were dead."

They had been Sarah Makin's flowers. Sarah Holroyd had no right to them.

Lifting her chin she smiled and crossed the room to stand beside him, trying not to look at the sinful nightdress.

The dream was giving way to reality. She was David's wife now and the big bed mocked her.

Turning her back, lowering her head, she whispered, "Unhook my dress, will you?"

Five

The great gates swung open, the lodge-keeper's wife bobbed a curtsey as they passed, and the fear that had smouldered uneasily in the deeps of Sarah's mind blazed into naked panic.

Now she had to face the music and it would assail her from all sides; from the people of the Three-streets who didn't easily forgive those who stepped out of line and from her husband's kind who didn't take gladly to a mill-girl with ideas above her station.

The train journey from Manchester in a first-class compartment had been most enjoyable. Indeed the whole morning, until this moment, had passed agreeably enough. Even awakening to the sight of her husband's head on the pillow beside her had not been unduly perturbing and to sip tea in bed as she watched him shaving was, she had had to admit, almost pleasant.

David had been kind to her last night, she conceded gravely, treating her gently, soothing her fears. For that at least she was grateful.

"I shall visit your father," he called from the dressing-room, "and beg his pardon for stealing his daughter so shamelessly."

"No!" she cried harshly. "He'll not see you. He took it badly when I told him about us."

"You didn't tell me that." David appeared in

the doorway, thoughtfully fastening his cravat. But there was a lot, he shrugged inwardly, they hadn't talked about. "Is that why he didn't come to the wedding?"

"It is," she admitted. "I didn't say anything because I thought it would be the same for you too. I didn't expect your parents would be over-joyed either."

"I see what you mean," he admitted. "To be honest, my father was away yesterday, in Liver-pool. He'd get to know about us when he got back, I shouldn't wonder. A bit of a shock, I suppose, hearing about your son's marriage sec-ond-hand."

"From the coachman, an' all," Sarah added soberly. "And what about your mother?" she whispered, wishing London were on the other side of the world.

"She'll get over it — they both will," he smiled. "Just give them time."

He kissed her gently and she closed her eyes, trying not to think of what might await them. It would not be easy, no matter what David said. Elders had contrary ways and there was no reason to suppose her husband's parents were in any way different. But best not dwell too deeply on such matters. Life had taught her never to court trouble since it could always find her with no bother at all. Later she would worry, not here in this unaccustomed place where everything had a dreaming air about it. And there was, she bright-ened, pushing aside her doubts, padding barefoot to the wardrobe, a most pressing decision to be made. Which, for instance, of these beautiful new garments to wear this morning? Would it be the fawn serge street-dress with its little matching cape or the velvet-trimmed skirt and jacket?

It should all, she yearned, be wonderful and exciting and dizzy-making. Then why, her head demanded perversely, was it not so? It was a question to which her heart could find no answer.

Now the unreal honeymoon was over and they were bumping up the drive to High Meadow in a hansom-cab.

Sarah had often seen the great house, but distantly, through locked gates, wondering what it would be like to have more beds than anybody could decently sleep in and fires that burned the whole day long in rooms that were never used.

Now it was her home and she was seeing it close to for the first time, this solidly built house of stone with a roof of no-nonsense slate and high, wide windows, a house little more than a quarter of a century old, yet which was mellow and perfect.

Sarah gasped at its beauty. Daffodils rippled in golden drifts in the woodland gardens and fat-budded rhododendrons made ready to greet the spring.

"Welcome to High Meadow," David smiled, helping her to alight.

She smiled uncertainly, walking catlike on the rough gravel. The sharp stones bit into her dainty shoes and she winced, wondering why she had so despised her solid clogs.

"It seems," David smiled wryly, "that we are expected."

A black-gowned figure appeared at the top of the stone steps, her hands clasped in front of her, a bunch of keys swinging from a belt at her waist. She inclined her head.

"Good afternoon, Mr David."

Sarah gazed dumbly at the housekeeper, then felt a shiver of dismay as she looked beyond the rigid shoulders and into the vastness of the entrance-hall.

Luke Holroyd stood there, thumbs pushed belligerently into his waistcoat pockets, feet slightly apart, his jaw clamped tight.

"Father!" David smiled easily, holding out his hand. "I didn't expect to find you home."

"I'll wager you didn't," came the dry retort, "but there's things to be said that won't keep, so I'd appreciate it if the pair of you would step inside."

He held open the door of his study, a room he had never learned to feel at ease in. It was a grand place, furnished with pieces wished on him by Charlotte's parents and packed with books no one ever read. He kept his study for brooding in and for occasions he found unpleasant, and his son knew it.

Placing his arm protectively round Sarah's shoulders David murmured:

"My dear, this is Parkes who looks after High Meadow for us. She will take you to my room."

His voice was firm, indicating that the altercation his father seemed set upon was men's business only.

The woman bowed stiffly and lifting a finger to summon a passing housemaid, gave clipped orders for Sarah's bag to be carried upstairs.

"Now, Father," David said quietly, closing the door behind him. "Which of us is to start this discussion?"

Luke's face crimsoned. He had not expected this quiet defiance although secretly he found it not unpleasing. The old man liked a fight, the more so when the protagonists were evenly matched. He had no time for men who cringed — never had — but his son had made him look a fool and for that he'd have satisfaction.

"This isn't a discussion," he said aggressively. "I want an explanation, lad, and it had better be a good 'un!"

"Then if that's all, sir, you shall have one. I told you, a week ago, that I intended to marry Sarah. I did just that, yesterday morning, in the parish church."

"That you did!" Luke roared, "without either your mother or me there, without family or friends or —"

"Or business associates and half the county set who couldn't give a damn, anyway," David finished mildly. "Be honest, Father. I did it the only way possible. Sarah wouldn't have countenanced a big wedding. She'd never have married me if I'd asked her to face up to such a ridiculous

110

charade. And that's exactly what such a wedding would have been!"

"Then why marry the lass at all, if you're ashamed of her? Is there some reason for this hole-and-corner affair? Have you got the lass into trouble, then? Is that what folk are to think?"

"People may think what they like!" David jumped to his feet, his eyes flashing anger. "If it's any of their business, I suggest they be patient and time will answer them. But get this clear, sir. I am *not* ashamed of Sarah. I love her dearly and I will not have her reviled by anyone. If you and Mama reject her, you reject me too. If she is not to be made welcome here then I will take her away!"

"Oh, aye? And what will you live on, the pair of you? Will you live on love, in a garret?"

"No, sir," came the steady retort. "I shall be well able to manage. There are mill-owners who would welcome my knowledge of postal selling. I could offer my services to Gideon Hindle."

"Hindle? That — that charlatan!" Luke gasped. "Have you taken leave of your senses? Work for my rival, for a man who'd sell his old mother's boot-laces if he thought it would turn a quick penny?"

"Gideon Hindle has a fine mill, father, with new machines and a sick-club for his workers."

"And you'd desert your poor old dad for him?"

"If needs be, sir."

The truculence melted from the mill-master's

111

face and his eyes took on the gaze of a down-trodden spaniel.

"Oh, the hurt of it," he moaned. "Was there ever anything so wounding as an ungrateful child? After all I've done." He swept his eyes heavenward. "After I've —"

"Schemed and slaved, worked your fingers to the bone?" his son suggested, eyes dancing. "Oh, Father, you should go to London, work the music-halls. You could render East Lynne to perfection. You'd have them weeping into their beer."

"By the heck, but you're a tough one under all that polish," Luke sniffed, abandoning his hurt, changing tack again. "You drive a hard bargain. You fight unfair."

"Yes, I truly believe I do," David admitted softly. "But I've learned it in the best of schools, haven't I? I'm a Holroyd."

A Holroyd? It dawned on Luke like the sun after rain. Of course the lad was a Holroyd! It had taken a time to show itself, but here was a new side to his son's nature.

Hope wrapped the old man in a warming glow. Happen marriage was going to be good for the lad.

"Ha!" he grunted, mollified.

"You'll receive Sarah kindly, then?"

"Aye. It might well be," Luke conceded, "that she'll do very nicely."

"She will," David smiled. "Oh, she *will*, I promise you."

"Then I suppose we'd better drink the lass's health."

Luke poured sherry, well pleased. By gum, he pondered, shaking with silent mirth, but this situation had the makings of a fine old to-do, be blowed if it hadn't. Caleb's lass versus Charlotte? Whatever the outcome, he decided impishly, life henceforth would not be dull. And on that he'd lay his last shilling!

The housemaid who carried Sarah's bag was pert and pretty and bursting with the importance of being the one to gain first-hand knowledge of the new Mrs Holroyd.

"Will you take tea, ma'am?" the housekeeper asked stiffly, "or will you wait until later? Mrs Holroyd will be taking hers in the drawing-room at three-thirty."

David's mother — back from London?

Sarah shook her head miserably. She didn't know how to speak to servants. They were so superior, so sure of themselves. Servants were not reduced to despair at the sight of a dinner-table or frightened silly at the prospect of fine living.

"Very well." The woman withdrew, motioning to the housemaid to follow.

Left alone, Sarah prowled uneasily around the room, picking up objects, putting them down again. She tried to interest herself in the photographs that lined the walls, but could not. They were all a part of David's past, a life about which she knew nothing.

Drawing aside the heavy lace curtain, she peered across the lawns to the parkland beyond. Down there, she supposed, lay Hollinsdyke, shut out from the beauty of the day by a blanket of smoke. And down there, straggling the canal-bank, were the Three-streets where her father lived and all her friends. Tonight they would go to the Mission Hall. They'd sit there as one and listen to another outpouring of Robey's anger. Folk stuck together in the Three-streets, Sarah yearned, wondering if she would ever dare set a foot there again.

Then she sighed impatiently and stuck out her chin. At this moment it was more important to know what was being said in Luke Holroyd's study. David had ordered her upstairs and she was grateful to him. She had not relished being the butt of Luke's anger.

Carefully opening the door, glancing either side of her, she walked softly to the head of the stairs, leaning over the banister-rail, listening intently, but there was no sound save the ticking of the clock that stood on the half-landing.

A door-latch clicked and Sarah spun round, flushing guiltily at being caught eavesdropping by a servant. But it was not one of those superior beings. Better by far if it had been, for there was no mistaking the tall figure standing in the door-way.

Sarah pulled her frozen lips into the shape of a smile, wondering if she should offer her hand or merely incline her head.

She was given no choice. Charlotte Holroyd swept along the corridor towards her like a galleon with full sails.

It would have been prudent, then, to have disappeared behind the safety of a closed door, Sarah considered, but wisdom had deserted her as she stood there, courting disaster, waiting for the fury to break around her.

But Charlotte Holroyd had better ways of dealing with the girl who had married her son. Satisfaction she would have — vengeance had to be slow and sweet. Drawing herself up with dignity, tilting her head so she was able to gaze down her nose, she stopped and faced her son's wife. For a moment she glowered down, then, lifting her lorgnettes to eyes that were little more than slits, swept her gaze over the trembling girl from top to toe, then back again.

"Tsk!" she clucked, as if she had beheld a troublesome insect. "Tsk!" Then brushing an imaginary speck of dust from the sleeve of her gown, walked on as if the younger woman did not exist.

Instinctively Sarah bobbed a curtsey, wishing the floor would open up and swallow her, then, picking up her skirts, fled to the shelter of David's room.

Tears pricked her eyes. She could bandy words with the best of her opponents and she could, if need be, give a good account of herself in a fair fight. But against open contempt she had no defence.

Miserably she slammed shut the door, then, throwing herself face down on the bed, pummelled the pillows with angry fists.

But she wouldn't cry! She *wouldn't!*

Uneasily Sarah dressed for dinner. Twisting her hair into a pleat she secured it with combs, then, patting her face with rosewater, dabbing lavender scent at her wrists, pronounced herself to be ready.

"You look very beautiful," David whispered, brushing the nape of her neck with his lips. She had chosen to wear the blue silk gown again and it pleased him.

"I'm afraid," she whispered. "I'll not know what to say and there'll be all those knives and forks to sort out."

"Then watch me and you'll be all right," he smiled, "and as for my mother — well, if you ask her about London, she won't stop talking, I assure you."

He made it all sound so easy, he who had been born into such luxury. And as for Mrs Holroyd, as for that formidable woman who had reduced her to a jelly with a glance, well, the likes of her didn't bear thinking about.

Sarah had not told her husband about the afternoon's encounter. It would have sounded childish, complaining about a look. But what a look it had been! She trembled, just to recall it. It embodied bitterness and dislike and total contempt. It had made her want to find a crack in

116

the floorboards and squeeze into it.

David offered his arm. "Shall we go down?" he asked comfortably.

Luke was standing beside the drawing-room fire and his eyes showed admiration as they entered.

"Well now. At last I get a chance to greet the bride." Placing his hands on Sarah's shoulders, he kissed her cheek. "Hullo, lass. That's a bonny dress you're wearing."

"David chose it," Sarah whispered, blushing at the unexpected compliment.

"Aye. David was always a good picker," he retorted obliquely, then turning to his son remarked:

"Cook's done us proud tonight. I believe the table looks a real treat."

Sarah accepted a glass of Madeira, grateful that Luke Holroyd at least seemed to have accepted the marriage. His attitude had thrown her off balance, for she had expected him to offer dire warnings of the perils in store for those who went to the altar without thought. She had not believed David when he assured her that all was explained and the explanation accepted. The mill-master was known for his guile, Sarah acknowledged apprehensively. Best she should take care. She made a mental note not to drink too much wine. Until last night she had never tasted alcohol. She had sighed the pledge almost as soon as she could write her name. The champagne they drank had made her lightheaded and this evening she had to keep her wits about her.

Instinct directed her glance to the open door and she caught her breath fearfully. Charlotte, splendid in lavender satin, was progressing down the staircase.

Sarah's stomach contracted painfully and she gulped hastily at her wine.

"Here's Mama at last," David smiled, taking Sarah's hand in his.

Charlotte paused in the doorway of the room, then, walking to her husband's side, tilted her cheek to receive his kiss.

"Evenin', my dear," Luke nodded amiably. "You look very smart."

"Tut! This old rag?"

She turned to greet her son, permitting him the smallest smile and a stiff inclination of her head. Totally ignoring Sarah, she said:

"Kindly tell Parkes we are ready, David."

"In a moment, Mama," he retorted softly. "I want you to meet Sarah. Please wish us well."

Shaking in every limb, Sarah offered her hand, but the older woman declined to take it.

"Sarah *whom?*"

"Sarah Makin, Mama," David supplied.

"One of the Lancaster Makins, perhaps? You'll be related to Sir John?"

"No," Sarah spoke slowly and quietly, remembering the softness of her mother's voice. "I live — lived — in Canal Street. My father is Caleb Makin and I was a weaver at Low

Clough before David wed me."

The words ended in a breathless whisper and she felt David's fingers tighten comfortingly around her own, heard him saying:

"Isn't she beautiful? Aren't I the luckiest of men?"

Charlotte stared down her nose, drew herself up tightly and murmured:

"Perhaps you will take me in to dinner, David?"

She laid her fingertips possessively on her son's arm, turning her back on the girl at his side.

"Mama!" His face flushed dully.

"A very good idea!" Luke intervened hastily. "And maybe Sarah will do me the honour."

His eyes met those of his son and signalled a warning. 'Not now. Not here. *Leave it!*'

"Of course," Sarah choked, finding it hard not to throw her arms around him and hug him from sheer gratitude. "I'd be delighted, sir."

Slowly the tension in the room dissolved and Luke let go his indrawn breath as the head-on collision seemed to have been averted.

"Drink up your wine, then we'll follow the others. Go on," he urged when she hesitated. "It'll calm you down — put the roses back in your cheeks. And if I may say so," he whispered, "I think that round went to you, Sarah Makin, so don't look so doleful. Chin up, eh, lass?"

The meal, as Sarah had feared, was a complete disaster. Not, surprisingly, because of the bewildering array of cutlery, crystal and fingerbowls, but wholly because of Charlotte Holroyd's studied rudeness.

At first Luke's wife declined to speak at all, concentrating on the food before her so there should be no doubting the strength of her displeasure. Then suddenly she laid aside her knife and fork.

"Well, husband," she pronounced in a high, clear voice. "I said it many times before and you made light of it, but I knew I was right."

"Right about what?" Luke growled, realising from years of experience that the tone of his wife's voice signalled trouble.

"About that quaint Lancashire saying, my dear," she said lightly. "How does it go, now? *From clogs to clogs in three generations.* Is it not about to come true?"

"Mama! Just what do you mean?" David's fork hit the table with a clatter.

"What I have in mind, I think, is something to do with the making of a silk purse." She stared meaningfully at Sarah. "From a sow's ear, of course. Pretty well impossible, I would say."

Sarah closed her eyes and shook with shame. How could David's mother be so cruel? Even in the Three-streets, folk didn't behave like that. They said what needed to be said without fear or favour, but they never used words as weapons.

From the serving-table came a gasp of amazement. The parlourmaid stood, ladle poised, her eyes popping, and the under-parlourmaid's mouth sagged open. The room was very still as, with an icy calm, David said slowly:

"Mama, I must ask you not to speak so to my wife. Your rudeness is most uncharitable."

The older woman gasped.

"How dare you?" she hissed, her cheeks flushing crimson. "I will not be reprimanded by my own son in front of servants!"

"And why not?" Luke demanded mildly. "Since everybody seems set on forgetting their manners, let's all join in. I think you've gone a little too far this time, Charlotte."

From across the room came the crackle of starched aprons and a hurried patter of feet. The servants at High Meadow knew when their presence was an embarrassment. The door opened and closed quietly.

"Well, madam?" With an exaggerated calm, Luke blotted his lips. "We are alone now, so maybe we'll hear your apology."

"No!" Sarah gasped. "Oh, please, *no!*"

But Charlotte was already on her feet and making for the door, her back stiff with indignation. She knew when to retire with dignity.

"Well, son?" Luke smiled wanly when his wife's retreating footsteps could no longer be heard. "There's a lesson in self-preservation, for you. Nine times out of ten, a woman's instinct is a very reliable phenomenon and best deferred to, but every so often a man has to assert himself. Tonight, lad, was one of those times. And maybe," he sighed, "it was as well to get things straight, right at the onset."

"I'm so sorry," Sarah choked. "It's all my fault. If I'd not come here, there'd have been none of this upset."

Her voice trembled and she stared miserably down at her hands. It was part of a nightmare. There was no other way to describe it.

"Oh, darling, it wasn't your fault," David hastened. "I never thought my mother could be so — so thoughtless. Please don't be upset."

"Upset? Of course the lass isn't upset!" Luke boomed. "I'll wager it'll take more than a tantrum to nettle Sarah Makin!"

Sarah tilted her chin. He was right. She wasn't made of pink sugar. She had married David for better or for worse. Tonight, she reasoned, was one of the testing times.

"Aye," she nodded, feeling the tension slowly slipping away. "I'm not easily put down. And if you don't mind, Master, let's get another thing straight. Sarah *Holroyd* isn't upset by tantrums either."

"By the heck, David lad," Luke roared, his shoulders shaking with laughter, "but you've found yourself a gradely lass, be damned if you haven't!"

Never, thought Sarah as fear slowly loosed its grip on her trembling limbs, had she ever thought to find an ally in Luke Holroyd. Strange, but if he hadn't been a mill-master, she'd have been prepared to swear he was almost human.

But everything was strange now. Nothing, she told herself silently, would ever be quite the same again. Nothing.

Sarah awoke with an uneasy start and peered, blinking, at the bedside clock.

Lordy! She'd overslept! Instinctively her hand touched David's pillow and it was cold beneath her fingers. This wasn't, she brooded, going to be a very good day.

Dressing quickly, she fought the panic that nowadays seemed never very far below the surface. She would be late for breakfast too. They would all be waiting there, drumming their fingers on the table, their eyes accusing.

She was pinning up her hair when she saw David's note and gasped with pleasure as she tore it open.

Sweetheart, she read,
I needs must work today, but I will be home early. Why not visit your father?
Please miss me a little.
                        D.

She smiled, strangely comforted, then ran hurriedly down the winding staircase. A maid in a blue cotton dress bobbed a curtsey as she passed and unnerved by such servility Sarah gasped:

"Am I too late?"

"For breakfast?" The girl sounded surprised. "Why, no, ma'am."

She indicated a door and bobbed again as Sarah nervously pushed it open.

It was a room she had not seen before, small and cosy with a fire burning brightly in the iron grate. Luke Holroyd sat alone, a napkin tucked beneath his chin.

"Hullo, lass. You've just missed David."

"I overslept," Sarah mumbled. "I'm sorry, but I seemed to lie awake till daybreak, almost."

"Deary me. Brooding, were you?"

"No. Just thinking, I suppose."

"Aye. It was only a storm in a teacup, last night," Luke said comfortably. "Nothing to fret over. Get yourself something to eat — we serve ourselves at breakfast." He nodded towards the side-table. "The kippers are very good."

Carefully Sarah lifted the lids of the silver dishes that stood on a warmer. Scrambled eggs, bacon, kidneys, kippers. Enough to feed a regiment.

Cutting a slice of bread she buttered it thickly then sat down at the table.

"Well, Sarah, and what'll you do with yourself today?" Luke demanded.

"I don't know," she admitted dubiously, realising that for the first time since she could remember she had nothing to do but please herself. "Maybe I'll go out, if I'm not needed here, that is."

"Which means that you intend keeping out of Mrs Holroyd's way," Luke commented dryly. "Well, I'd not worry overmuch, if I were you.

Like as not she'll spend the day in her room, making plans."

"Plans?" Sarah whispered.

"Planning how to spend my brass. When David's mother is aggrieved, it comforts her to spend money. Likely she'll be off again tomorrow, either to her sister Clara's in Cumberland or to visit the cousin who's married to a Scottish earl, or back down to London again. Charlotte isn't fond of Hollinsdyke society," he sighed.

"But this house is so beautiful. If it were mine, I'd never want to leave it!"

"Wouldn't you, lass?" Luke's eyes gleamed with pleasure. "You like High Meadow, then?"

"Like it? Why, it's like something out of a storybook. But it's a big place," she added dubiously, "for such few folk to live in."

"You're right," he admitted. "But I didn't think so, when I built it." His eyes took on a faraway look. "I built this house for a family, Sarah. I wanted sons in it and bonny little daughters. I wanted to fill it with noise and happiness." He shrugged, looking down at his plate. "Folk in Hollinsdyke used to walk up here on Sunday afternoons to watch it being built. Luke's Folly, they called it behind my back, but I took no notice because I knew one day they'd envy me my big, roistering family. But I worked my fingers to the bone for a dream." He laughed shortly. "I should have known that in real life, dreams have no substance."

Sarah glanced at the rough-hewn face. The

hardness was gone and in its place lay sadness. Could this man be misunderstood by those who lived in Hollinsdyke's small streets? Could he, underneath, be deserving of pity?

Pity for a mill-master? From Caleb Makin's daughter?

"Had you considered, Sarah," Luke broke into her thoughts, "that one day this house will be yours to care for? Will it bother you that likely they'll call you Mistress of Luke's Folly?"

"I hadn't given it a lot of thought," she hesitated, taken aback. "This marriage came about so suddenly that sometimes I still can't believe any of it."

"You mean you've never wondered what it would be like to be lady of this house?" He looked at her quizzically, one shaggy eyebrow raised. "I'm surprised, yet I'm inclined to believe you. I'll admit, though, I thought you'd had an eye to the main chance. But, if you didn't, then why did you marry David? And in such a hurry too."

Sarah shrugged and regarded her fingers, as if, somehow, the strange gold band there would provide her with an answer.

"I don't rightly know," she hesitated.

She really didn't know. She had done it in a fit of pique. She had rushed in, unthinking, like she always did.

"Do you love him, Sarah?"

"No," she whispered flatly. "No, I don't think I do. But I respect him and I'm grateful for his kindness," she hastened. "I promised to be a good wife to him and I'll stand by it."

She hoped her answer would satisfy him, even though it might not be the one he wanted to hear.

"Then tell me — are you truly a wife? Are you wedded and bedded, Sarah?"

The question was startling in its directness and she floundered for words.

"If you mean can you hope for grandchildren," she whispered, "then the answer is yes. One day there'll be the bairns you want about the place. Does that please you?"

"Aye, Sarah. It does. It pleasures me a lot," he replied huskily. "I'd give most of what I own to know there'd be Holroyds in this house when I've been called to my Maker. Only give me grandchildren, lass, and you shall have anything your heart could want. I swear it."

"I want nothing, Mr Holroyd," she said evenly, "except maybe an apple-pie."

She was rushing in again, but the Three-streets had taught her to grasp every passing chance.

"An apple-pie?"

"The one left over from dinner, last night. There was a large dish of trifle too and a fruit-cake. All those things for afters and all sent back to the kitchen, untouched. What will become of them, do you think?"

"I don't need to think," Luke replied darkly. "I *know*. They'll be eaten in the servant's dining-room, that's what."

The appetites of his servants had always been

a thorn in Luke's flesh.

"And how many of them are there?"

"Eight in all, counting outside."

"So they do pretty well?" Sarah reasoned. "They'd not miss that pie, I shouldn't wonder."

"Now see here, Sarah," Luke exploded, un-used to such quizzing. "Be blowed if I know what you're getting at. What do you want with an apple-pie?"

"I want to take it to the mill-school, Mr Hol-royd, *your* school. I want to give it to your ap-prentices. And I want soup for them, every working day and bread to eat with it."

"Soup and bread? Free? *Out of my own pocket?*"

"If needs be. Those children are hungry."

"But I give them work," Luke fretted. "They get their money, regular, every settling day. And tell me, whose was the only mill in these parts to keep working during the American troubles? When they were fighting each other and there was no cotton grown, who alone but me gave work to the people of Hollinsdyke?" he de-manded triumphantly.

"The American War's been over for years," Sarah flung disparagingly, "and cotton's cheap again. Think about it," she wheedled softly. "Why, word of your generosity might even reach the Queen's ears. And you'd be spiking Robey Midwinter's guns," she added slyly. "He's got it in for you, Robey has. Says you work your ap-prentices —"

"I know what he says," Luke ground. "And I

haven't lost any sleep over it."

"All the same," Sarah persisted. "Soup and bread and leftovers from your table? It's nothing to you, but you'd be blessed by those children every day. And it'd please the good Lord, I shouldn't wonder . . ."

Luke pursed his lips and narrowed his eyes. Happen she was right, at that. *Do unto others? Suffer little children?* And the Lord might indeed be pleased, bless him with grandchildren of his own.

"How much," he hesitated, rubbing his chin thoughtfully, "will all this frivolity cost me, do you suppose?"

Sarah laughed triumphantly. Maybe it wasn't going to be such a bad old day, after all.

❧

"Wait for me," Sarah instructed the coachman. Her heart was beating uncomfortably, but sooner or later, she had reasoned, she had to show her face in Hollinsdyke. Besides, she had pressing business to see to and news she was bursting to impart, so best get it over with.

The mill-school was housed in a side-street, well away from the mill. Once it had been a run-down weaver's cottage, but Maggie Ormerod had scrubbed its floors and whitewashed the walls and even persuaded Luke Holroyd to supply coal for its iron stove. She was cleaning the blackboard when Sarah pushed open the door. For a moment she hesitated, then, holding out her arms cried:

129

"Sarah! Oh, how grand you look!"

Then they were in each other's arms, hugging and laughing as old friends do, with no barriers of class or riches between them.

"It's good to see you, Maggie love," Sarah whispered huskily, delighted by the warmth of her welcome, wishing she could dislike Maggie, glad she could not.

"You'll take a cup?" Maggie set a kettle on the stove top. "The children aren't due until one o'clock."

"It's about the children I've come," Sarah hastened, anxious not to be sidetracked into talking about the wedding. "See what I've brought."

She nodded towards the basket and from the folds of crisp white napkins took an apple-pie and a fruit-cake.

"These are for the children, Maggie. There was a trifle too, but I wasn't in time to rescue that. They'd got it eaten," she said sorrowfully.

Maggie flushed with delight. "Oh, Sarah. They'll think it's Christmas!"

"Then from now on it'll be Christmas every day," Sarah laughed, "because, starting tomorrow, there'll be soup and bread for all the apprentices and anything else I can find. What do you think to that?"

"Every day?" Maggie gasped. "It's so good of you, so kind . . ."

"Nay, it's on Mr Holroyd's orders," Sarah smiled, knowing the more credit she gave to Luke the better the apprentices would eat. "It was him told me to arrange it. I'll try to bring it myself, each day. It'll be good to have a chat, see Billy-Boy. And, Maggie," she hesitated, "will you keep an eye on father for me? He's a stubborn old cuss and he'll have nothing to live on now but the few shillings he makes from his potions." She held out a sovereign. "Here's some money. See that he gets a meal now and then. No need to let him know it's come from my purse."

"I'll do that gladly," Maggie promised, "and I'd let you know at once if ever he got sick. Did he take badly to the wedding?" she ventured.

Sarah nodded. "Nothing pleases him these days. But I'll visit him on his birthday. Maybe he'll have got over the worst of it by then. After all, he can only turn me away."

She smiled, but there were tears in her voice. Her father was old and sick in body and mind, but she remembered when he had been the handsomest man in the Three-streets and her mother the most ladylike of women. They had laughed a lot in those days.

"I'll have to go, Maggie. We can have that tea some other time."

She was worried, truth known, about the coachman. It was past dinnertime and he'd want to get back to High Meadow. It wouldn't do, she worried, to keep him waiting.

"Tomorrow I'll stay longer and have a chat with Billy-Boy. I miss him," she sighed. "Give him a hug sometimes, Maggie."

Another minute and she would have missed

the man. She would have been driving up the street in the carriage and she could have pretended not to have seen him. But it isn't possible to ignore a man who's tall as a tree, with shoulders so broad they block the doorway. Oh, why had he come here?

"Robey," she whispered, her heart quickening at the sight of him.

"Why, if it isn't the lady from the big house, Mistress Holroyd herself, come slumming in Hollinsdyke!" He touched an imaginary forelock then bowed with an exaggerated gesture. "Or has Sarah Makin come to show off her fine feathers in the Three-streets?"

"Robey!" Maggie admonished. "That's not fair! Sarah came with food for the apprentices and they're to have soup regularly now — every day."

"Is that so?" He raised an eyebrow, his lips pulled down in a smile of disbelief. "Is Milady Bountiful trying to ease her conscience, then? Is she sorry for deserting her own kind? By the stars, Sarah Makin, I thought you'd more about you than to creep off and sell yourself cheap to a mill-master's son!"

Sarah stood as one who has turned suddenly to stone. To see him so unexpectedly had been shock enough. To have to withstand his derision was almost unbearable.

The man who smiled into her eyes and gave her primroses was gone. The Robey in whose arms she had wanted to lie no longer existed. To her eternal shame she had longed for that man, yet now lie lashed her with contempt, looked at her as though to touch her would soil his hand. He made her want to clench her fist and lash out blindly. She wanted to hurt him as he was hurting her but he had rendered her incapable of such passion. White-faced, she walked to the door, then, turning, heard herself whisper:

"I'm sorry, Mr Midwinter, if I've upset your plans, but from now on I promise you'll have no cause to complain about the way in which the apprentices are treated."

She said it softly with a ladylike calm her mother would have been proud of and she walked to the carriage with a dignity Charlotte could not have bettered. But there the deception ended. Safely out of sight, she gave way to the tumult inside her.

Damn the man! Why did she find him so good to look at? Why did she want a man who despised her so?

Closing her eyes tightly, she bit on her clenched fist until she winced with pain. She hated Robey Midwinter! She loathed and detested him! Be damned if she would let him make her cry!

But, for all that, the tears that streamed down her cheeks were hot and bitter and all the way back to High Meadow her body shook with silent sobs.

Would she never get him out of her mind?

Six

Maggie Ormerod placed her hands together and bowed her head.

"Bless our food, Lord, and make us humbly grateful for the charity of our betters."

"Amen." The response was ragged and impatient.

"All sit."

The apprentices needed no prompting. Spoons clattered, eyes closed blissfully. The soup was thick and hot, the bread plentiful. Such bounty was almost unbelievable and they ate quickly, lest it should be snatched from them.

"A hungry bairn is a terrible thing," Sarah choked.

The school-teacher nodded soberly. She worried about her orphans constantly. That Sarah proposed to feed them made her dizzy with delight, so who cared if folk in the Three-streets muttered that Caleb's lass was heading for a fall? Sarah could rub shoulders with the devil himself, so long as Maggie's pupils reaped the benefits.

"There's more to follow," Sarah smiled as each bowl was polished clean.

It was fortunate, she admitted, that Charlotte Holroyd's cook was one of twelve children whose artless concept of heaven had been stew and dumplings four times a day and bread and jam between times, doled out by a smiling Archangel Gabriel. Cook had not only provided soup, she had made a large currant pasty too.

"You're a good soul," Sarah whispered soberly, silently thanking Providence for a woman who still remembered the pangs of a hungry child-hood.

The pasty was eaten with sighs of delight and when every crumb had gone, every finger licked, Sarah prepared to leave. Here, in the little class-room, she had been able to forget the vague worries that preyed upon her mind. She had felt at ease, and grateful that Maggie had not asked one curious question about the secrecy and haste of the wedding.

"I'd like to talk to Billy-Boy," Sarah said as she packed the hamper. "But not here, not in front of the others."

"Then leave your gloves behind," Maggie suggested. "I'll send him out with them."

When the door opened and Billy-Boy stood hesitant, gloves clasped in a small, thin hand, Sarah held out her arms, smiling happily. She had missed him and the sudden luxury into which she had been pitched served only to emphasise the dreariness of the little boy's life.

He came to her reluctantly and Sarah felt his body stiffen as she hugged him to her.

"Don't you love me any more?" she teased. "Have you forgotten your Sarah already?"

"You went away," he choked. "You didn't tell

me. I waited and waited . . ."

"I went to get married," she smiled gently, "but I'm back again. I shall see you almost every day. It'll be the same as it was before, won't it?"

The child nodded dubiously. Sarah was a fine lady now and rode in a carriage. He'd liked it better when they worked together at the looms. Now he had to share her and it worried him that one day she might stop coming. But the food she brought had been good and he felt duty-bound to tell her so.

"I liked the soup," he said shyly. "Will there be more tomorrow?"

"Of course there will," she choked. "Sarah won't forget you."

Anger and compassion struggled inside her as she climbed into the carriage. She had to do something to help Billy-Boy. She had to take him out of the workhouse and out of the mill, see him apprenticed to a craftsman who would give him a home and treat him kindly. David would arrange it. David, who refused her nothing, would make it possible.

The idea pleased her. Where was the sense in marrying into money if she was to forget those she was in a position to help? She could help her father too, if only he'd bite on his cussed pride and let her.

Oh, imagine, she yearned, in the bogey of Charlotte's resentment could be banished and her father would give his blessing to the marriage, how pleasant life could become. But her mother-in-law's displeasure was as real as Caleb's stubborn hatred of anything that bore the name of Holroyd and it would not be easy, she sighed.

But she had made a start. The mill children need never go hungry again and soon she would have Billy-Boy's future settled. If only Robey Midwinter would take himself off, out of Hollinsdyke, out of her thoughts.

She shook her head impatiently, angry with herself for thinking of the man as she did. But his mocking eyes haunted her constantly and even in the private darkness of their bedroom, with David's arms around her and his lips gentling hers, she could never quite shake herself free of that dark, handsome face.

She was a fool; a complete and utter fool and one day, she prophesied darkly, she was going to be sorry for her self-inflicted stupidity.

Oh, why, she sighed, had she been born so perverse? Why did she have to complicate her life so?

Life was becoming complicated for Luke Holroyd too. He had awakened to a bright spring morning and felt near-contentment as he drove to Low Clough. He had been pleased that Sarah had given him full credit for the providing of the apprentices' victuals and mildly grateful that Charlotte appeared to be staying in her room to nurse her injured pride. He had just filled his pipe and taken out last month's Profit and Loss Account — the most pleasurable reading he knew

— when Albert Dinwiddie appeared at the door, wearing a face that foretold trouble.

"Have you a minute, Mr Holroyd?" The counting-house manager's face was flushed and it was obvious he was the bringer of news. "Nay, I'll not sit down," he gasped as Luke indicated a chair. "I've not got long. They'll be here any minute!"

"*They?*" Luke scowled.

"Aye. They've stopped work in t' spinning-room to discuss it and likely the weaving-shed'll join 'em afore long. They're drawing lots for a spokesman. They've got a grievance and they're coming to see you."

"They've alus got a grievance," Luke growled as his bright spring morning darkened. "What is it this time, Albert?"

"I don't rightly know, Master, Silk seemed to think it's over the to-do last night. I suppose you know there was another meeting at the Mission Hall and —"

"And Midwinter was crying stinking fish again," Luke supplied. "Don't tell me any more!"

He raised his eyes heavenward, sending smoke to the ceiling in short angry puffs, silently imploring his God to bear witness to the tribulations that beset a mill-master.

Robey Midwinter was becoming a nuisance, he brooded, wondering whether to stand firm on his dignity or whether to accept the challenge the rabble-rouser seemed intent upon hurling.

"Get back to the counting-house, Albert," he

138

advised, "and say nowt. Leave it to me."

Dinwiddie scurried along the passage, duty done. Closing the door of his little office he mopped his face. Normally he was never unduly alarmed by day-to-day upsets that were only to be expected in any cotton-mill, but this time he had sensed unease when Silk brought details of the gathering in Tinker's Row. Mill-workers always grumbled. Some of them had even joined the trade union, but their resentment usually blazed fiercely and burned out quickly.

Now it was different. Midwinter had come to Hollinsdyke with a great deal to say. And they listened to him. He was a man's man that women sighed over; he was dangerous, and best left to Mr Holroyd, Dinwiddie decided, popping a mint humbug into his mouth and champing it furiously. And may the best man win!

The deputation straggled across the mill-yard and clattered up the counting-house stairs. Luke saw them coming from his window and calmed his ruffled feelings by breathing in deeply then exhaling through stiff, indignant lips. It made a hissing sound that put him in mind of an angry gander. The simile pleased him and added to his determination not to yield an inch.

One of the tacklers had been elected leader. Pulling off his cap he wished Luke a respectful good-day.

"And what seems to be the trouble?" Luke demanded, when the five men had arranged themselves around his desk.

"I'm come to tell thee, Master," the man cleared his throat awkwardly, "that there's grievances in t' mill. We want guards putting on t' machines and more money for our pains. And there's bairns in the shed not nine years old —"

"Then they are the most fortunate of infants to be working at Low Clough," Luke smiled smoothly, "because from now on they'll be given good victuals, every working day. And entirely at my own expense, mark you!" Luke delivered his trump card with relish. "What have you to say to that, eh?"

"I say that soup for fifteen childer costs nothing!" a sallow-faced spinner took over the discussion. "I say it's been done to pull the wool over our eyes."

"It was done out of the goodness of my heart," Luke protested mildly, "and shame on him that doubts my good intentions."

Again the cunning old eyes implored the heavens to mark his sincerity.

"And shame on you, Master! You pay us starvation wages. The men over at Syke Mill get a ha'penny an hour more'n us and we want the same!"

"Then you'd better walk the three miles to Syke and see if you can get taken on," Luke suggested amiably. "Be reasonable, now. A ha'penny an hour?" He swept the men with disbelieving eyes. "Have you stopped to work it out? Don't you realise that to do as you ask would

140

raise your wages by three whole shillings? Can't you see that that would cost me an extra thirty pounds a week?" He spread his hands in a gesture of bewilderment. "Now where's a man to find money of that magnitude?" he appealed.

Blinded by such calculations it appeared that no one could provide the answer until a small, wizened man suggested:

"Happen the women-folk'd make do with a farthing."

"A farthing an hour to all the females I employ?" Luke gasped, "when they're already on a bonus on their yardage?"

"And which most of them are hard put to it to make," flung another. "We can't manage on what we get and that's the truth, Master. Some of us have a lot of mouths to feed."

"Then there's the answer to all your problems," Luke smiled as though suddenly all was explained. "Don't have so many bairns!"

Slowly he rose to his feet and, taking his top-hat from the peg behind the door, placed it firmly in position.

"And now, if you'll excuse me, I have a pressing business engagement." He gave a good-natured nod of his head to the gaping assembly. "And rest assured that I shall instruct Mr Dinwiddie not to make any deductions on settling-day for time lost this morning. Bid you good-day, gentlemen."

He walked sedately along the passage, head erect, then crossed the yard to where his carriage waited, his countenance radiating goodwill to all men. He sustained the expression until he was well away from Low Clough, when anger stained his cheeks scarlet and evil intent swept the benevolence from his face.

A ha'penny an hour, indeed! Damn Robey Midwinter and his interference! Who was he, this trouble-maker who refused to be ignored? Where did he come from and who was behind him?

The Master of Low Clough did not know, but he'd find out, so help him, and before very long, an' all! Master Midwinter had gone too far this time!

David smiled reassuringly at Sarah across the dinner-table. He never tired of looking at her and tonight, with candleglow reflected in her eyes and the anxious little hollows in her cheeks accentuated by the flickering flames, she was so beautiful that his heart ached dully.

She had seemed happier, more relaxed, as they dressed for dinner, chattering about her plans for the mill-school, but when he suggested the time had come to visit her father the animation left her face and her body tensed visibly in protest.

"Not yet, David. The time's not right. Leave it to me."

"But, Sarah, it is impolite of me to make you my wife and not acknowledge your father. I want him to know I shall take care of you. And he must be lonely now. He likes the lanes and the hill tops, you say, and there are empty cottages on High Meadow land. Why don't we offer him one?"

"Oh, please *no!* He's a bitter man," Sarah pleaded. "He'd sooner live in the workhouse!"

"Very well. We'll leave it for a time," David yielded. "But sooner or later I must visit your father. Civility demands it."

He regretted having upset her, the more so since without warning his mother had chosen to leave the confines of her room and take her meal in the dining-room.

Sarah's eyes showed alarm as the older woman took her place at the head of the table, accepting the formal bows of the men with a small smile, inclining her head in Sarah's direction as if acknowledging an unwanted guest to whom she must needs be polite.

From then on the conversation had become brittle and forced and Sarah ate little, praying for the meal to end.

But by some miracle, or maybe it was Luke's meaningful gaze in Charlotte's direction, the tension at the table did not explode into bitterness and Sarah's misgivings became a little less acute.

There could be no denying, she conceded, that Charlotte was a remarkable woman. Born into the ruling classes, she was only exercising, Sarah supposed, her divine right to rule. She had no warmth or tenderness as her own mother had had, but she was real, nevertheless. Somewhere inside her had surely to be the capacity to love.

Sarah sighed, self-pity washing over her. She

had never ceased to miss her mother, even though such longings had been kept in check, and it would have been nice, she yearned, to have been able to talk to David's mama, learn from her.

The doors opened quietly and the housekeeper rustled the length of the room to stand beside Luke's chair, her hands in the familiar clasped position.

"What is it, Parkes?" Luke demanded, slicing irritably into the cheese. He disliked having his meals interrupted and his shaggy brows met in a frown.

"There is a person asking for you, sir. He came to the back door. I told him you were not able to see him but he insisted I inform you of his presence. His business, it would seem, is urgent and confidential."

"Oh, aye?" Luke glowered. "And does this person have a name?"

"It is a Mr Silk, sir."

"Something's wrong?" David looked up sharply.

"It wouldn't surprise me," Luke conceded. "Trouble and Silk are never far apart. I don't know why I bother with him," he sighed, reaching for the decanter. "All right, Parkes." He dismissed the housekeeper with a nod. "Show him into the study when I ring."

"What do you suppose he wants?" David demanded. "Could it be anything to do with this

144

morning's upset, or could it be the gypsy?"

"The gypsy?" Charlotte arched her slender brows.

"That's what they're calling the rabble-rouser, it seems. There's a man," David explained, "who is telling our workers how badly done-to they are. It seems that nothing will content him but the complete disruption of Low Clough. Midwinter's his name. He's a born talker and a bit of a mystery package, by all accounts."

Sarah drew sharply on her breath and looked down at her fingers.

"And the gypsy is worrying you, husband?" Charlotte's laugh tinkled falsely.

"Not so's you'd notice," Luke growled, "though I don't take any too kindly to being told how to run my own mill."

"Then how providential it is that I have decided to visit my sister," came the smooth reply. "I do so dislike trouble and perhaps by the time I return, Luke, you'll have sent this gypsy fellow packing."

"I don't doubt that I shall," Luke retorted dryly, rising to his feet. "Perhaps you'll excuse David and me. We'd better see what Silk has come about. After all, my dear, he might have come to tell me that Low Clough's on fire!"

"No! Oh, please never joke about such a thing!" Sarah gasped.

She closed her eyes as an icy finger touched her. Her father had used similar words, but Caleb had not joked.

*I'd give most of what was left of my life to see
Low Clough go up in smoke!*

Her father meant every word, Sarah thought,
dry-mouthed. They had issued from his lips like
a prayer to the devil.

"Don't worry, Sarah." David was on his feet
in an instant. "Father's sense of humour takes a
little getting used to. Drink a glass of wine; it'll
do you good. Silk's visit will be a fuss over nothing, you'll see."

"No thank you." Sarah waved away the decanter. "And I'm not upset, David. Not really . . ."

It wasn't true, but in no way would she wilt
or wither in Charlotte Holroyd's presence.

"Then happen you'd like to come with us,"
Luke suggested. "After all, it's mill business and
the sooner you see the other side of the coin,
Sarah lass, the quicker you'll grasp what you've
taken on. There's more to being a Holroyd wife
than living up here in splendid isolation!"

The words were uttered with resigned bitterness, but Sarah was quick to catch that Luke
directed them at his wife, for she saw the flush
that stained the other woman's cheeks and the
slight flaring of her nostrils.

"That's a fine idea!" David enthused, grasping
at any excuse to separate his mother and his wife.
"Sarah's opinion might be useful, Father."

And so it was that Sarah sat uneasily in a corner
of the study, preparing to learn mill-business

from the other side of the divide.

Aaron Silk sidled in, his hat clutched between his hands.

"It's good of you to see me, Master," he gasped. "I came at once. I thought you should know before morning what was afoot. I took the liberty of acquainting Mr Dinwiddie with the facts and he agreed that forewarned is forearmed, as they say."

"You make it all sound most alarming," David remarked. "Is something wrong at Low Clough?"

"Not yet, Mr David, but there will be. There was another meeting at the Mission Hall tonight. Most of Low Clough was there, although the ringleaders came mostly from the rabble of the Three-streets."

Sarah bit her lip angrily, marvelling at Silk's impudence. Either he didn't know that she herself was sprung from that rabble or he was a very stupid man. Her eyes met David's and she saw with relief that his own were filled with laughter. Taking her cue from him, she relaxed. Silk was a fool, anyway. Old Luke would use him only as long as it pleased him. When his tale-telling lost its value he'd be thrown aside for the parasite he was.

"And?" Luke prompted. "Get on with it, man!"

"They're going to give you one more chance, Mr Holroyd. Midwinter says they must ask you again to raise their wages and if you won't they'll strike."

147

"Will they, by heck? And where's that going to get them? Where's it going to get any of us? What'll they use for sustenance? Is this man going to work a miracle? Is he going to support them with fine words when they've nowt in their pockets? Haven't they realised that talk is cheap?"

"I think you should have Midwinter arrested, father," David flung impatiently. "He's inciting people to disobedience, maybe violence . . ."

"Nay, lad. Not so fast. Don't get carried away. Nothing was said about violence, was it, Silk?" Luke questioned pointedly. "Midwinter'll not counsel anything like that. From what I've heard about him, he'll not overstep himself. If he hasn't incited law-breaking, there's nothing I can do about him." Luke knew what he was about. "Oh, if only once he'd step outside the law."

"I can't say he did anything wrong," Silk admitted. "The man seemed reasonable."

Silk had seen or heard nothing that could be used against the gypsy. Tonight there had been no mockery in his voice, no derision, no challenges. They were no longer necessary. His audience had long since been captivated. They were ready now, to follow every whispered suggestion, latch on to the smallest innuendo. Robey Midwinter had stormed the citadel. Now the people of the Three-streets were eating from his hand.

"Mr Holroyd will listen to you," he had urged with sweet reason. "Of course he's refused your request. They always do, the first time. But ask again, and ask humbly. Luke Holroyd was a

148

spinner once. He'll remember."

"He'll remember nothing!" had come the angry reply. Luke Holroyd's forgotten the likes of us. He lives up there in that great house of his and thinks he's almighty God!"

"Then remind him," Robey insisted gently. "Appeal to his better nature. No man can be so base that he turns his back on the roots he sprang from."

"That man'ud turn his back on St Peter at the Gate, if it suited him!"

"Oh my friends. Be charitable. You *will* prevail." The man they called the gypsy had held out his arms in a gesture of benediction. "You, my hungry ones, will inherit the earth!"

My, but he was clever, Silk thought. He would give old Luke a run for his money, all right. It would be a wise man who could forecast the outcome of this to-do. A wise man indeed . . .

"So what's to be done?" David demanded when Silk had left. "This Midwinter is dangerous."

"I know it," Luke grumbled, "and it isn't the only thing I'm bothered about. There's five mills in this town and heaven only knows how many more, all over the county. So why did he pick on *my* mill?" He thumped the desk-top angrily. "And who's harbouring him? If we knew that, it would be a start."

He looked directly at Sarah and she met his stare blankly. It wouldn't help any to tell him and anyway Silk would find out soon enough.

"Sarah — I know this must be painful to you," David placed his arm around her shoulder, "but have you any knowledge of this man?"

No knowledge, husband, her heart cried. Only an upset inside me whenever I am near him, only the need to gain his approval, the need, if I am truthful, to feel the touch of his hands on my body, his lips . . .

"No!" she replied sharply. "Why should I? Does anybody know who he is?"

"It's all right, lass. I reckon you're as mystified as we are," Luke nodded, "only I've got to say this, Sarah. You're a Holroyd now. You'll bear it in mind, won't you?"

Ah, yes, and in return for such a privilege, she accepted silently, she would outwardly conform. She'd play fair, but in her heart she would be Sarah Makin, still, the weaver who tended four looms and fought like an alley-cat at the dropping of a challenge. The secret Sarah would always be there.

"I'll bear it in mind, Father-in-law," she whispered.

And I will be two people, she thought fearfully. I will be torn apart by duty and inclination. No matter what happens, I shall always understand the people of the Three-streets. If Life should scratch any one of them, Sarah Makin's foolish heart will bleed.

She was up early next morning.

150

"Can I ride with you into Hollinsdyke?" she asked her husband over the breakfast-table.

"Indeed you may," he smiled. "But why so early?"

"I'm going to see my father," Sarah hesitated.

"Then I heartily approve. It will pave the way for my own visit. Do you want to take him a gift, Sarah? Have you sufficient money?"

"I'll take him some tobacco, and I've more than enough money."

Guilt squirmed inside her at his trusting goodness. True, she was going to see her father but for what purpose she couldn't have told. She genuinely wished to see him. Her conscience had not ceased to plague her since the day he stormed, hurt and bitter, out of the house. But there was more to it than that, even though she couldn't decide exactly what it was.

"I've seen Cook. If I'm not back in time, she'll see the food is taken to the school. It's barley broth today," she smiled, "and jam buns for a treat. Cook is a good woman. She doesn't complain at the extra work."

"And you are good, Sarah." He reached for her hands and held them tightly. "I love you so much, my darling," he whispered. "But you know that, don't you? You know I'd die for you . . ."

"David! Please? You mustn't say things like that! Maybe I'm a superstitious mill-girl, but *please*, never say that again." Suddenly the room had lost its brightness and warmth. There was a heaviness in her heart, a suffocating weight on her chest as if someone danced a jig on her grave. "Promise me?"

"I promise, my funny Sarah."

Could it be, he wondered, that she was beginning to care a little?

Sarah waved to her husband as the carriage drew away. She had asked that she be set down at the top of Tinker's Row. It wouldn't have done, not this first time, to be seen arriving in so grand a manner.

She carried gifts — a twist of tobacco and a packet of peppermints, but her heart beat uncomfortably and she had to school herself to walk with indifference.

No one called out a greeting. It was as if they had known she was coming, she thought miserably, and shut their doors on her.

Her father was pounding roots for boil-salve when she walked into the kitchen. Its smallness shocked her. She had been left the little house for less than a week yet by comparison with High Meadow's loftiness it seemed even more mean. Caleb knew she was there, but he did not look up.

"So you've come, my proud lady?" he mocked.

"Aye, Father. Sarah's come."

"To show off your fine feathers, I don't doubt. Had you forgotten I said you'd not be welcome here?" His lips were twisted with bitterness.

"No, I hadn't forgotten," she whispered, will-

152

ing her hands not to tremble so. "But I was passing the top of the street. I couldn't walk by —"

For the first time Caleb raised his head and looked directly at his daughter. His face was blank as a slab, his jaws tight with distaste.

Meet me half-way? Sarah's eyes pleaded.

"Why have you come?" the old man muttered. "Do you want to shame me?"

"I've done nothing to be ashamed of, Father. I'm decently wed."

"You call bedding with a Holroyd decent? You allow yourself to be kept by the man who brought me to *this?*" He flung out his arms in a gesture of hopelessness, his twisted limbs grotesque. "You can forget my sufferings?"

"Father, it's done now. Let the past take care of itself. I'm married too and that can't be changed either. Accept it."

"Are you happy, then?" The question was reluctantly asked.

"I'm happy enough. David wants to come and see you. If you'd accept him I'd be a lot happier."

Caleb resumed his pounding, turning his back as if there was nothing more to be said.

"Tell me — what is Robey up to?" Sarah whispered. "He doesn't know what he's about to start. Tell him to go, Father. Ask him to leave us in peace."

"Us? Who do you speak for, daughter? Have your new masters sent you? Are they getting worried?"

153

"No-one sent me," she retorted wearily. "Luke Holroyd can look after himself without any help from me. I wanted to make sure you were all right. You're my father. It worries me that Robey Midwinter is out to cause trouble."

"Then don't worry about me. Don't worry about any of us in the Three-streets, Mistress Holroyd. The only trouble there'll be will be for you and yours. Robey'll take care of the likes of me. It'll be the mill-masters who'll be screaming for mercy, afore much longer!" He spun around, laughing, yet his face was set in a mould of triumphant hatred. "Take yourself back to the fine folk on the hill. We've no liking for turncoats in these parts. Go back to that folly Luke Holroyd built. And may he burn in hell!"

"Father," Sarah pleaded, suddenly afraid. "There's enough unhappiness in the world without you and me adding to it."

But Caleb was staring into the fire, deaf to her pleading. Placing her gifts on the table she choked:

"I shall come again on Monday. I haven't forgotten it's your birthday."

Tears stung her eyes and she dashed them angrily away. She had been wrong to come. Her visit had served no purpose but to widen the chasm between them and to prove beyond all doubt that her flimsy fears had taken on a frightening substance.

Her father was beyond help, there was no doubting it, and his last bitter words rang in her ears as she strode the road that led her back to High Meadow.

May he burn in hell! It was the curse of a madman.

Seven

The Holroyd pew in Hollinsdyke parish church was carpeted and cushioned but Sarah wriggled with discomfort for every eye in the congregation was turned in her direction.

Once, when she was little, she had sat beside her mother in this very church and gazed upward in awe at the fine family who sat in isolation to the left of the altar, rubbing shoulders, or so it then seemed, with God Himself. She had wondered about the mill-master and his high-born wife, weaving fantasies around them, imagining how grand it would be to sit there in glory beside the fair-haired boy who was as beautiful as the cherubs on the painted ceiling.

Now, amazingly, that boy was her husband, and rubbing shoulders with the Almighty, she found, was an unnerving experience. Indeed it was so discomfiting that she was glad when Matins was over and she was able to seek refuge in a corner of the carriage.

"An enlightened sermon, don't you think?" Charlotte enquired of her husband.

Luke grunted and leaned back in his seat. The message from the pulpit had been too long by half and he'd been hard put to keep his eyelids from closing.

"The vicar enjoys the sound of his own voice,"

he grumbled, "and he's forever begging. Asked me only yesterday for money for the orphanage. As if there aren't enough demands on my re- sources," he added petulantly, remembering the demands of his workers for a rise in their wages. "I told him he'd better put the matter before the Ladies' Charity."

"Which means he'll be asking *me*," Charlotte flung tartly, "and just when I had almost decided to send the proceeds of the Charity Ball to the fund for Missionaries."

The Charity Ball was the great event in Hol- linsdyke's smug social calendar. To be sum- moned to attend was the next best thing to shaking the hand of the Prince of Wales and those who were favoured to receive Charlotte's gold-edged invitation counted themselves fortu- nate and gave gratefully to her Charity Fund. Everyone whose pedigree was acceptable to Charlotte and the ladies of her committee, and could be relied upon to give generously, attended the ball in the Assembly Rooms. Sarah knew all about the Charity Ball; she should do, for she had always watched the arrival of the guests from behind the broad shoulders of an officer of the law. To witness the comings and goings was an event never to be missed by the womenfolk of the Three-streets. It was the next best thing to the mayor's parade.

Now, Sarah realised, she too would go to the ball. She would arrive in a carriage with a maid in attendance to fuss over her gown; she would walk up the broad sweep of steps to the Ohs and Ahs of onlookers.

Sarah Makin had come a long way, she thought soberly, since she had fought Poll Clegg in the Low Clough yard. It was almost unbelievable and very frightening. It was as if she were still seated on the roundabout, still riding the prancing horses, only now they were whirling faster.

The ball was a grand occasion and she would make a fool of herself, she thought miserably as the carriage swung into the drive that wound through the trees to High Meadow. She would say the wrong things and do the wrong things and David would be ashamed of her. She wondered if she might plead indisposition on the night, have a sudden attack of vapours or a make-believe fever. Unfair perhaps, and deceitful too, but better than facing the slanting stares, the raised eyebrows, the heads that would nod behind fluttering fans.

Later she spoke of her fears to her husband. They were walking in the garden, the smell of newly cut grass heavy on the air, the sun warm in the sheltered corner where already a white magnolia bloomed.

"I don't think I want to go to the ball," she announced. "It's got me bothered, thinking about all those grand folk."

But David had laughed and taking her hand in his, squeezed it tightly.

"Don't worry, my darling," he whispered. "You'll be so beautiful that the men will envy me and the ladies turn green with jealousy."

"But I shall do something wrong," she insisted. "I don't have fine manners and I use all the wrong words when I get flustered."

"Oh, my lovely Sarah," he shook his head in fond exasperation. "Don't try to be something you're not. Be your dear self, and everyone will love you. And you shall have the grandest gown of them all. We'll go to Manchester and order one. In the palest pink and scattered with rose-buds, I think it must be; cut low to show your shoulders."

Sarah sighed. There was to be no getting out of it. For some strange reason David thought she was beautiful, imagined that all men desired her as he did. She would have to attend, if only because of his kindness. And he *was* kind and good, her conscience stressed and she *didn't* de-serve him. She should be married to a man who would beat her regularly and make her polish his Sunday boots, a man like —

She shut down her thoughts at once. She wouldn't think about Robey Midwinter. He wasn't the only man who was tall as a tree and so handsome it disturbed her, just to look at him. The world was full of men like him and they all added up to trouble. Those who were stupid enough could listen to his silver tongue — he wasn't fooling *her!*

"What are you thinking about so earnestly?" David demanded, breaking into her guilty thoughts so that she blushed scarlet.

"Oh, I — I was thinking about the Charity Ball, I suppose," she floundered. "I was thinking about speaking to your mother, asking her if she'd tell me what was right and wrong," she flung, off balance. "She could teach me how to act like a lady," she rushed on, warming to her lies, "how to speak —"

But David pooh-poohed the idea, then traced the outline of her face with the tip of his finger.

"No one," he whispered, "need teach you anything. Anyone as beautiful as you needs no social graces."

His eyes searched hers, loving and desiring her and she turned her head away sharply as he bent to kiss her.

"Not here, David!" she hissed tartly. "The servants might be watching!"

It was a pompous thing to say, she knew it at once, seeing the sudden alarm in his eyes. She didn't know why she had said it. As if a kiss mattered.

"Sarah," David ground as, embarrassed, she turned to walk away. "Never speak like that to me again!" His voice was sharp with reproach and she knew she had hurt him. "You sounded," he said, shaking his head as if lost for words. "You sounded just like Mama!"

They laughed about it afterwards as they walked arm in arm toward the house.

"Minx!" David scolded after she had kissed him until he forgave her. "I really thought you meant it."

160

But she had almost meant it, Sarah admitted. She had wanted to copy Charlotte Holroyd's manners and social graces, to know what to say and when to say it, be proud and haughty, as she was. She needed to be able to ape the older woman's brittle coldness, shield herself from attack, if needs be. There was much she could learn from the proud lady of High Meadow, Sarah decided, if only it could be possible to break down the coldness between them, talk together as women so that in time they might at least call a truce. It was up to her herself, she thought, to make the first move. What could be lost by offering her friendship to David's mother? Wouldn't it be worth a try?

"Now what are you thinking about so secretly?" David demanded. "What new notion is buzzing in that head of yours?"

"Why," Sarah retorted, wide-eyed. "I was only thinking about my beautiful new ball-gown."

She closed her eyes briefly, disliking herself, promising tonight when she said her prayers to have a good long chat with the Lord about her impious ways. It was becoming alarming, she brooded, the way untruths seemed able to spring unbidden to her lips.

"And I was thinking about your mother too," she added. "Just a little . . ."

Luke dismissed the carriage then picked his way across the puddled yard. He was not in the best of spirits. Monday was his least favourite day, a wet Monday even more so. And that was not the least of it, for the moment he entered the mill-yard he had felt the unrest. The mill was working as it always was when he arrived, punctual as the clock, at half-past eight each morning. The chimney belched smoke and scattered soot, the looms clattered and cotton bales swung high on the spinning-room hoist. To an outsider it was normal enough, but the man who owned Low Clough, who understood every stick, stone and mood of it, knew better. He sensed the tension, smelled the discontent as if it were a slow-burning fuse. It was as if eyes pricked into the back of his neck, as if the mill itself had joined the brooding displeasure and marked his passage from a hundred watching windows.

Luke tensed his shoulders and walked with deliberate slowness toward the counting-house stairs. It was no surprise that Dinwiddie was waiting there, changing feet like an agitated sparrow, hands twisting.

"Mornin' Albert. What's up, then?" Luke slammed his hat on the peg. "What's bothering you?"

"It's nowt to do wi' me, Mr Holroyd," the counting-house manager exploded. "It's that yellow-faced tackler from the spinning-room, him 'as came to see you, wanting more money. Told me to ask if you'd see the deputation —"

"I've seen 'em," Luke barked. "The answer was No, then, and I've had no cause since to change my mind!"

". . . if you'd see the deputation *again*. Said as how they wanted to do things fair and square, like. Said you'd reconsider, he was sure, you being a reasonable-minded man," Dinwiddie finished with a gasp, the message delivered.

The silence in the room was thick. Luke rested his elbows on the desk-top and glowered at the wall clock. Dinwiddie mopped his brow and moistened his lips. The upset was not of his making yet he was being growled at by both sides.

"Well, Master?" he croaked. "What am I to say?"

"Say I'm busy, Albert. Tell them you delivered the message but that I'll be busy all week — oh, you know what to say!" he finished testily.

"Aye, Mr Holroyd, I do. In a word, the answer's *No!*"

Luke smiled grimly and nodded, then settling his spectacles on his nose, unfolded the morning paper with exaggerated calm. The interview was over.

Dinwiddie sighed and left, closing the door behind him with a kind of gentle fatality. At the clicking of the doorsneck, Luke pushed aside the paper and cocked his head, listening to Dinwiddie's retreating footfalls, then, taking out his watch, began to count.

A minute would be all it would take for Dinwiddie to tell Silk and for Silk to scuttle across the yard with the reply. In just a few seconds it would all be over and done with and they could forget the nonsense.

Footsteps in the passage outside caused Luke to smile and he walked to the window in time to see Silk heading at break-neck speed for the spinning-room door.

Luke snapped shut his watch and replaced it in his waistcoat pocket with seven seconds to spare.

"By gum," he chuckled, "but bad news travels fast!" Then settling himself in his chair again, filled his pipe with tobacco.

A ha'penny an hour indeed? Whatever was the world coming to?

Charlotte Holroyd made her final choice of dinner-dresses from her wardrobe, added a mere half dozen tea-gowns, then declared herself satisfied. Now her clothes could be packed and she could set out for Cumberland and the home of her sister Clara. Charlotte had considered visiting her cousin, the countess, but the Scottish castle in which she lived was damp and dark and the earl's table frugal. Cumberland would suit her better for a few days, she decided, and then she would be back, to approve the final arrangements for the Charity Ball.

She clucked impatiently as the door-knob rattled, then stiffened visibly as her son's wife entered the room.

"Can I talk to you?" Sarah whispered.

"Have we anything to say to each other?" Charlotte demanded.

"Yes, ma'am, I think we have. This is a barn

of a house but no place is big enough for two women at odds with each other," Sarah said quietly. "I want us to be friends. Won't you give me a chance? Help me?"

She held out her hand, willing her mother-in-law to take it, pleading silently for one small act of kindness, one charitable word. She had known that at first there would be difficulties, but surely every woman wanted a daughter just as she, Sarah, had never ceased to want a mother. A truce would make life so much more easy.

But the hand she offered remained unclasped and the older woman turned coldly away.

How dare she? How *dare* this girl set her cap at David, inveigle him into marriage then expect to be treated as an equal? And how dare she wreck the carefully laid plans of a mother who wanted only the best for her son?

"Help you?" Charlotte flung. "I would suggest you are well able to help yourself!"

"But I only want you to teach me a few airs and graces so I'll not let David down at the ball," Sarah frowned. "I don't want to let anybody down," she added hastily, "but I'm not used to such grand affairs, you see, and —"

"Then you should have stayed within your own habitat," Charlotte ground, "married someone of your own station in life and left the choice of my son's wife to *me!* Oh, I dread to imagine what people must think."

Sarah's cheeks flamed as she fought down the anger that blazed inside her, praying silently that just this once she might not lose her temper.

"You mean they'll say the marriage was forced on your son, that I'm having a baby?" she demanded.

"And aren't you? What other reason could there be for so disastrous a marriage?"

"No ma'am, I'm not. Life's hard enough in the Three-streets. We don't look for trouble."

"Then why did you come here? Why did you force your way into this family and by what right do you demand I should even acknowledge you, let alone try to make you into a lady?" The words were acid, for she had grown bitter with discontent. At odds with life, she had seen no reason over the years to add to the happiness of others. "I don't wish to speak to you," she added flatly and finally. "Please leave my room!"

It would have been better, Sarah thought miserably, if David's mother had struck her; such an injury would have been easy to forget. But words could wound deeply and their hurt lingered longer because they left no bruise or scar. Suddenly she felt alone and defenceless and the bewilderment that screamed to be heard burst out in an indignant torrent.

"Oh, I'll go," she flung. "It was foolish of me to come. I wasn't trying to ape my betters, act like I'm a lady born like yourself, but I did want you to like me. Is that so very wrong? And I wanted a mother again — someone to share woman-talk with, someone I could turn to if I was bothered. I wanted it so much," she choked.

For a moment the tears inside her welled into a constricting lump in her throat and she stood trembling, unable to speak. Then the girl from the Three-streets tossed her head in defiance. Wrenching open the door she hurled her parting shot.

"But don't think *I* care! If my mother'd been alive she'd have taught me. My mother spoke like a lady and she knew how to behave in genteel company. *She* worked for the gentry, at Ainderby!"

"What's that, girl?" Charlotte's head jerked round. "Did you say Ainderby?"

"That I did!" Sarah retorted. "My mother mixed with better folk than this town'll ever know. Lords, ladies — she served them all. She'd have taught me how to conduct myself in company. Why, they had such grand balls at Ainderby, just to hear about them would make your hair curl! You'd never believe it, if I told you!"

"Oh, but I would," came the whispered reply.

How *could* she? How *could* this girl awaken memories, Charlotte fretted, conjure up days long gone? By what right did she reach into the shadows, remind her of a happiness she thought she had forgotten?

Unwillingly she looked afresh at her son's wife. Standing there, she admitted, was she herself almost thirty years younger, a girl sick with delight at the thought of an Ainderby ball; a girl young, brash, heedless of her elders' advice and desperately in love with William — penniless

William who had asked her to marry him in the rose garden at Ainderby. It had been at the coming of age of the eldest son, she remembered, with everyone there. They had danced until morning came and she'd given her heart into William's keeping.

"You've heard about Ainderby too?" Sarah whispered. "Then it wasn't just a fairy story my mother made up?"

"It was real, child, and it's like a fairy story remembered, a dream . . ." Charlotte mused, her eyes far away, her heart suddenly young, beating as it had done so many years ago with the love of being alive.

"And was there a grand ball like my mother said, and did all the young ladies creep away from their chaperons and meet their sweethearts in the garden? It did happen, didn't it?" Sarah pleaded.

She wanted so much to hear it again, for just a while to be a little girl again, with a gentle-voiced mother who knew so many lovely things.

"It happened," Charlotte nodded. "I know it, for I was one of those young ladies. I remember that we always prayed for our chaperons to nod off, so we might escape. On the night of the ball my old chaperon drank too much wine and fell asleep in her chair and I ran down to the rose garden . . ."

Dear William, who had sailed for India to seek his fortune so he might marry her and who died there, of cholera, the man who still held her girlish heart in his hands.

"I can't believe it," Sarah gasped with delight. "You were at that ball? You were truly there? Oh, it *was* a wonderful place, wasn't it, just like Mam said?" She couldn't bear it, if it hadn't been.

"Your mama was right, Sarah. It was an enchanted place and nightingales sang that night and the world was so very beautiful . . ."

Tears trembled on her voice as the past became the present and she recalled that young, heart-broken Charlotte who was bullied into a marriage she hadn't wanted, and memories of the heartache faded from her thoughts as she remembered again that past love.

Sarah closed the door and walked slowly to the side of the woman who was no longer to be feared. Sinking to her knees, she was a child again in the kitchen at Canal Street, listening to her mother's gentle voice. And the kettle bubbled on the hob, ready for when Caleb, her handsome father, came home from the mill.

"Tell me," she pleaded softly. "Please tell me about Ainderby."

David found them there in the firelight, his mother and his wife, sharing something too special to be interrupted. Mother and daughter you'd have thought they were, he mused, closing the door gently again, walking quietly away.

Dearest Sarah. She had charmed his father and now she had found her way into his mother's unhappy heart. She was irresistible and lovely and so dear to him that it hurt when she wasn't near him. She gave herself to him without protest, lay passive in his arms, yet he knew she did not love him as he loved her.

Something, someone, he pondered, was keeping her from him. If only he knew, he frowned, what or who it was.

The problem was still with him that evening as they sat together in the small drawing-room. It was a cosy, lamplit room and they had taken it for their own.

"Mama's good humour seems to have returned," David remarked, relieved that the barriers between the two women seemed at last to be coming down, wishing he could have shared, or even understood, the closeness between them.

"I think," Sarah retorted cautiously, "it is because she is pleased to be visiting her sister."

"And I think not. You have found your way into Mama's affections just as I knew you would. What mischief were you plotting? You were so engrossed, the two of you, that you didn't even notice me."

His voice was teasing but his heart was uneasy. He too wanted to be close to Sarah, share small intimate confidences with her. As a wife, she could not be faulted. She was obedient, eager to please him, and he should be the most contented of men. But some part of her eluded him, he brooded. The Sarah he had first loved, that exciting creature with her hair blowing free and a wildness about her that flamed his senses, evaded him even yet.

"Mischief?" she smiled. "It was only gossip, woman-talk."

She couldn't explain that they had been brought together by longing, that the past had reached out and linked them. She couldn't admit that deep inside them they had both searched for affection. She, Sarah, had yearned for a mother's love, but for Charlotte it was the remembered kiss of a long-ago love that gentled her heart into compassion.

"Talk," Sarah stressed. "About the ball."

"I see. You were planning what to wear? You'll have to hurry. It's little more than two weeks away and you haven't yet seen the dressmaker."

"I shall wear pink, as you suggested," she retorted, unwilling to explain it had been another ball she and Charlotte had talked about. Will you help me choose a style? Shall we go tomorrow?"

"We shall indeed." He could refuse her nothing, and the familiar longing for her swept over him again. Without doubt, she would be the most beautiful woman at the Charity Ball. With her black hair pulled into the nape of her neck and the exquisite whiteness of her shoulders enhanced by a low-cut gown, she would captivate every man in the room.

"She is mine!" he would want to shout. "This lovely creature is my wife!"

And she was truly a wife, he frowned, yet, even as she lay gentle in his arms, there was still a part of her that remained impassively remote.

"Do you realise," he demanded, pushing aside the thoughts that disturbed him so, "that you will be the belle of the ball? Men will rush to sign your dance-card. It will be filled twice over, I shouldn't wonder and I shall be the most neglected of husbands."

"Oh, but you needn't be," she retorted. "Just to think of it sends me into a bother. What will I say to all those grand folk? And another thing —" Her lips tilted in a half-smile. "Did you ever stop to wonder if I could dance?"

"But *can't* you, Sarah?" he gasped. "I thought everyone could dance."

"Now how," she flung, "could the likes of me learn such things? Mill-girls don't go to balls and anyway dancing was frowned on at the Band of Hope. Downright sinful, they said it was although I often thought I'd like to try it. But how can you dance the waltz," she sighed, "in clogs?"

"Oh, my dearest Sarah," David laughed, gently cupping her face with his hands. "You are such a contradiction, such a joy to know!"

His lips found hers, his gaze unashamed in its desire.

She closed her eyes at his kiss, caring for him yet ill at ease. Why did her heart have to be so wayward? Why couldn't she love him, just a little, in return?

"And you, David," she retorted gravely, "are a good and kind man and I am grateful for all you have done for me."

172

It was not the answer he wanted, the sudden pain in his eyes told her that, and she disliked herself at once for hurting him so. Why was she so stupid, so unthinking? Why couldn't she count her blessings and thank heaven for the love of a good man?

Impulsively she sank to her knees before him, then taking his hands in hers she whispered:

"Please give me time. I'm trying so hard. Be patient, David."

He smiled and kissed her again, knowing he would never cease to want her. Gratefully she melted into the shelter of his arms. And she would try, she vowed silently. *She really would try.*

They were walking hand in hand up the staircase when the urgent ringing of the front doorbell caused them to pause.

"Who can it be?" Sarah whispered, apprehension tingling through her. "It's late . . ."

The footman who always answered after-dark calls walked slowly across the hall below them as the bell clanged again.

"Wait here," David ordered tersely, running lightly downstairs. "I'll see to it."

When the door was opened Sarah was unable to distinguish the man who stood there, but her doubts were dispelled when a voice demanded:

"I'm here to see Luke Holroyd. Tell him it's Robey Midwinter!"

She caught her breath in a gasp as the familiar

weight pressed down on her chest and ghouls danced on her grave again. Here was Trouble, searching them out.

The footman stood aside as David called: "Come in, sir. My father isn't here, but if I can help . . . ?"

"Nay, I'll bide where I am. I'm not here on a polite errand and I'll not hand you the satisfaction of having me thrown out. But if the organgrinder won't see me, then I'll make do with his monkey. I take it I'm speaking to the young master?"

His words were thick with sarcasm and Sarah's apprehension turned to anger. She disliked people who used words as weapons and Robey Midwinter was altogether too good at it. Clenching her jaw, she ran quickly down the stairs and took up her stance at her husband's side.

"What do you want, Robey Midwinter?" she demanded, her voice low with outrage. "You're not welcome here. Go back to wherever you came from!"

"Leave us, Sarah!" David's voice was harsh as he pushed her behind him. "This man's business is *my* concern!"

"Aye, Sarah. Do as you're bid," Robey mocked. "He's right. My business doesn't concern you any longer, though maybe you should stay and hear what I've got to say. Happen then you can persuade your new masters to heed my warning."

His eyes swept her from head to toe, flashing

contempt, his lips slanting derisively, then, turning to David, he said:

"The workers at Low Clough have asked for another ha'penny an hour. They've asked it twice and been refused. I'm serving notice that unless the master sees fit to grant that request inside seven days, the workers will withdraw their labour, as is their right!"

"Strike, you mean?" David ground.

"Call it what you like," came the comfortable report. "It'll all be the same in the long run. There'll be no more yardage, come Saturday night."

"And no more money either — had you thought of that?" David flung. "How long can they live without money?"

"As long as it takes," came the arrogant reply. "Just as long as it takes to convince you that God is not a mill-master!"

The seconds stretched into eternity as they faced each other in brooding silence, then, pulling off his cap. Robey touched his forelock in an exaggerated gesture of servility and, sweeping a low bow, smiling as he said it, wished David a pleasant goodnight.

"And you too, Mistress Holroyd," he whispered. "May your dreams be sweet and your conscience rest easy beside you!"

Then throwing back his shoulders he turned abruptly and strode away.

The darkness instantly wrapped him round and they stood, unmoving, listening to the crunch of

175

his feet on the gravel of the drive. Only then did Sarah give way to the pent-up emotion inside her.

"Oh, David," she whispered, her voice harsh with fear. "Please do as he says. It isn't much they're asking and it'd be a small price to pay."

"Pay, Sarah? For what? Are we to be blackmailed by this gypsy, give in to his whims without a fight? Who is he?" he demanded, "and by what right is he so familiar with the use of your name?

"By no right at all," she retorted wearily, "except that he knew me by that name before I married you. It means nothing. It's just the way he goes about things, that's all."

"You seem to know a great deal about him." His voice was cold. "How long has he been in Hollinsdyke? How long have you known him?"

"About as long as I've known you," came the whispered reply. "I met him the day you offered me a position in the counting-house though it seems, sometimes, like a lifetime ago."

"Is that the truth?"

"I give you my word." She raised her eyes to his and her gaze was steady.

And she *had* answered him truthfully, she urged as they walked once more up the broad sweep of stairs. She had first met Robey the day she'd fought with Poll Clegg in Low Clough yard. Thank the dear Lord David hadn't asked her why she had stood there trembling at the sight of the man, or why her heart had turned over at the sound of his voice. To have answered such

176

questions truthfully would have been another matter.

"Please believe me," she urged, taking his arm, hugging it tightly. "You mustn't get strange ideas into your head. I'm your wife, David, and I care for you."

"Do you, Sarah? But how much do you care and how much of yourself do you keep hidden from me?"

For the rest of the evening there was an unkind silence between them. Bewildered, Sarah prepared for sleep behind the closed door of the dressing-room and when she crept into the bedroom her husband did not open his eyes or turn his head on the pillow.

"Good-night," she whispered to his unyielding back as she turned down the lamps and pinched out the bedside candle. But he remained uncompromisingly aloof and he did not whisper to her in the darkness or reach out for her.

A noise in the courtyard below awoke Sarah and she jumped guiltily out of bed, peering through the curtains to see Charlotte's trunks and boxes being loaded into the carriage.

"Lordy! This would happen!" she fretted, splashing her face with cold water, dressing hastily. Yesterday David's mother had unbent and shown kindness and it would be uncivil, Sarah reasoned, not to be there to wish her goodbye.

Charlotte was sitting in the breakfast-room

177

when Sarah burst in, red-faced and flustered.

"Good morning, ma'am," she gasped, praying fervently that the goodwill of the previous day still held good. "I'm sorry — I slept late."

Charlotte nodded stiffly to a chair, then pouring a cup of tea and handing it to Sarah said:

"I am afraid that yesterday we allowed ourselves to be carried away by sentimentality which is rarely a good thing, and not to be encouraged. Nevertheless I enjoyed our chat and when I return next week we will talk about the Charity Ball. And Sarah — never, *ever,* come down to breakfast with your hair undressed!"

Sarah let go her indrawn breath in a gasp of relief. It was going to be all right. Given time, they might yet become friends.

It was only later, when she sat alone, munching bread spread thickly with Cook's special lemon conserve, that Sarah was able to take stock of the situation.

Last night, for the first time, David had shown jealousy. There had been a coldness between them and this morning he had left for the mill without awakening her.

And it was all Robey Midwinter's doing. Robey had no right to come to High Meadow, threatening a strike, using her name with deliberate familiarity, making a downright nuisance of himself. That she found him disturbing was a matter only for her conscience, but the man had become a threat to the people of the Three-streets and

178

something had to be done. For everybody's peace of mind, he had to be persuaded to leave Hollinsdyke.

She said as much to Maggie Ormerod as they ladled soup into the apprentices' waiting bowls.

"You should know, Maggie — what's behind it all?" Sarah demanded. "There's been upset in the place ever since Robey came. Doesn't he realise the damage a strike will do?"

"Mister Holroyd wouldn't stop the children's food, would he?" Maggie asked anxiously. "If the mill came out, he'd not be so cruel as to take it out on the apprentices?"

"No." Sarah shook her head firmly. "The bairns won't suffer, I promise you. I only wish, though, that Robey would leave us in peace."

"He'll not do that," Maggie sighed, cutting thick slices of bread. "His mind's set on getting something done at Low Clough. It's not just the wages — he's right about the machines too. They're dangerous — but you know that, don't you?"

Tight-lipped, Sarah nodded. She didn't need reminding. The day her father had been carried home still lived vividly in her memory.

"I'm not defending Luke Holroyd," she whispered, "but there's better ways than striking to get things done. Surely they know the old man won't be pushed?"

She patted Billy-Boy's head as she prepared to leave and slipped a twist of humbugs into his pocket, brooding guiltily that she still had not spoken to David about taking the child out of the workhouse, finding him a kindly home. But there had been so much to do. Folks would never believe what a time-consuming business it was, being rich and idle.

But speak to David she would, she resolved, as the sad brown eyes gazed up into hers.

"Will you come again tomorrow, ma'am?" Billy whispered solemnly.

"Aye, child. Sarah'll look after you."

She would too. She would speak to David about Billy this very night. Setting the world to rights wasn't easy — miracles never were — but at least she must find the time to make one small boy happy. Whatever happened, she had not to fail Billy-Boy.

Kissing Maggie warmly, Sarah sighed and picked up her basket. She wasn't at all sure what she would say when she got to the Three-streets, for her heart had begun to beat uncomfortably just to think about it. But today was her father's birthday and it was the excuse she needed to warrant another call at the little house that backed on to the slow-moving canal. She knew she would be greeted coldly, treated with contempt, even, but it would be worth it if it enabled her to talk sense to her father, get him to warn Robey Midwinter that his actions could lead to nothing but trouble.

She called out cheerfully as she entered the house, despite the foreboding that warned her to turn and walk away. Her mouth was dry and her heart thumped so loudly she feared her father must have heard it.

But it wasn't Caleb who rose straight and tall from the fireside chair and she bit hard on her lip to prevent herself from crying aloud.

"Why, good-morning, ma'am. If it isn't the young mistress from the Big House come spreading her bounty again!"

Sarah turned away, fighting down the tumult that thrashed inside her. Playing for time, she placed tobacco, bacon and a freshly-baked loaf on the table top.

"Bid you good-day, Robey Midwinter," she whispered. "I'm here to wish my father the compliments of his birthday," at once furious with herself for stooping to explain her actions. "Where is he, do you know?"

"Gone to Market Street to deliver a potion for whooping cough," he supplied. "I'd not wait, if I were you, Sarah. You'll not be welcome."

"But you are *not* me!" she flung, trepidation giving way to anger, "and I'll thank you to mind your own business. What's more, I'll wait in my father's house as long as I've a mind to and, if my being here bothers you, you've only got to leave!"

"Do you want me to leave, Sarah? Do you *really* want it?" His voice was low and indulgent and his eyes challenged her to tell the truth.

"Of course I want it!" she gasped. "I want you to leave this house, this street. I want you to go away from Hollinsdyke and never look back! Oh, why," she pleaded, "did you have to come here?"

He took a step toward her and stood so near that she could hear his rasping breath. Dismayed, she dropped her head, tensing her body in an effort to still the trembling that shook it from head to toe.

"I came to right a wrong," he whispered. "I told you that, the night we walked together over the hills, the night before you wed the mill-master's son."

"And what wrong might that be?" she jerked.

"You know it as well as I do, Sarah Makin. Oh, why are you so contrary? Why is every word you utter a nonsense of cussedness?" He grasped her arms roughly and swung her to face him. "And why didn't you think on before you wed David Holroyd?"

His eyes blazed into hers, his nearness sent her giddy with longing and she wanted to feel his arms around her, his mouth hard on hers. But he had called her contrary and cussed and besides she was David's wife. Breaking from his grasp she rounded on him like a wild cat.

"Then why did you let me?" she sobbed. "You knew you had me bothered. You picked me flowers, that night. You'd only to say —" She stopped, her breath shuddering in her throat.

What was the use? Robey was Maggie's and she, Sarah, wasn't free to love him.

"Go away, Robey," she moaned. "There'll be no peace for this town while you're here."

"And for you, Sarah?"

"No peace for me either," she choked.

"I'll go when my work is done and be glad to," he jerked, "for you torment me as I never thought to be tormented again. But before I go I swear you'll remember me!" and gathering her into the circle of his arms he held her close, kissing her eyelids, her cheeks, gentling her body until her resistance was overcome and she relaxed, crying softly against him.

"I want you, Sarah Makin," he choked. "I wanted you the moment I laid eyes on you."

His mouth found hers roughly and she was too weak to resist him. He kissed her again and again, until her head reeled and every small pulse in her body beat madly with need of him.

"Robey, oh, Robey . . ."

A little keening sob escaped from the secret deeps of her heart and the cry shocked her. It was the cry of a wanton, the animal mewl of unbridled need. Through the mists of her madness she heard her husband's voice,

'Dearest Sarah, you are such a joy . . .' and self-disgust swept over her. Tensing her body against him, tearing herself from his arms, she stood like a cornered animal, panting and weak, her eyes flashing a warning. Pulling the back of her hand across her mouth she gasped:

"Leave me alone! Don't touch me! Don't ever touch me again, Robey Midwinter!"

Sobbing, she flung past him, out of the house, into the street where cool air hit her like a slap to her face.

What had she done? What new madness had she let loose and what would be the outcome of it? She had wondered about Robey's arms, longed for the feel of his lips on hers, and now she knew.

They wanted each other with an intensity that was frightening and she had never, ever, to let herself be near him again. She had to close her ears to the sound of his voice and close her heart against the memory of his kisses.

Biting on her knuckles, she began to run. The cobbles were sharp beneath the soles of her dainty shoes and the pain gladdened her, reminding her that her loyalty lay no longer in the Three-streets. She was Sarah Holroyd now and she had to remember it always.

But another man's kisses still burned her lips and her heart beat madly with the remembrance of his closeness and even as she neared the gates of High Meadow her body was still a torment of unsatisfied need.

"Dear heaven," she whispered. "What will be the end of it?"

Eight

Sarah wandered in search of company, her footsteps echoing behind her in the emptiness of the house. She liked the warm, homely kitchen with its smell of scrubbed tabletops and she liked Cook, whose big brown teapot was always at the ready.

She smiled, recalling the delights of Senor Umberti's warehouse in Manchester, the swish and rustle of silks and satins, the velvets, soft to her touch.

She had spent the morning choosing materials for her ball-gown and cloak and to add to her enjoyment David's good humour seemed completely restored, the coldness of the previous night forgotten. And that, Sarah supposed, had been entirely due to the sense of guilt which had prompted her to behave more lovingly towards him. Indeed the shame she felt at the remembrance of Robey's kisses had made her go out of her way to make atonement for her slide from grace and to vow, yet again, to banish him from her mind.

Cook was relaxing, her feet on the fender, enjoying the peace left behind by Charlotte's departure.

"I got the victuals off, ma'am," she remarked

comfortably. "Sent them down in the tub-cart with the stable-lad."

"You're a good woman," Sarah smiled. "One day soon you shall come with me to the school and see for yourself how the children enjoy your cooking."

"Aye, hunger's a wicked thing," Cook sighed, "and that's not the worst of it, if all I hear is true."

"What did you hear?" Frowning, Sarah set down her cup.

" 'Twas the stable-lad told Mrs Parkes. Had it from the school lady. One of the apprentices got hurt this morning — lamed on a machine strap."

"At Low Clough?"

"So it seems," Cook nodded reluctantly. "But happen someone got it wrong in the telling. No cause for you to go fretting, ma'am."

No cause at all, Sarah thought uneasily, but people didn't make mistakes about accidents in the mill.

"I'm going to Hollinsdyke," she whispered. "Will you send someone to the stables, please? Tell them I want the carriage — quickly!"

She took the stairs two at a time, her heart pumping dully, and, flinging on a cape, was waiting at the front door long before the carriage arrived.

"Take me to the mill-school," she cried, wrenching open the door, dismissing the coachman's attentions with impatience. "And *hurry!*"

Leaning back against the cushioned interior,

she closed her eyes and tried not to think. But the memory of the dreadful day from her childhood would not be pushed aside and she lived again through another accident, saw her mother's face, pale with shock, and her father's fine body, made hideous by one of Low Clough's machines.

Now it had happened again, this time to a child, and it had to stop. If Luke Holroyd would do nothing, she vowed, then David had to be made to. Somehow, those great clattering looms had to be made safe.

The mood in the schoolroom was subdued. Small heads jerked up as Sarah entered.

"I've just heard!" she gasped. "Is it bad? Who's hurt?"

Maggie Ormerod's eyes were red-rimmed and her lashes spiky with tears.

"Oh, Sarah. It's Billy," she whispered.

"No!" The breath left Sarah's body. "Where is he? I must take him to High Meadow. He must be properly nursed!"

Stunned, she was stumbling to the door when her arm was grasped with unaccustomed roughness.

"Sarah! Stay here! There's nothing you can do. There's nothing any of us can do. He's dead. Billy's *dead,* do you hear?"

"Dear God." The words left Sarah's lips in a terrible moan and her eyes wandered aimlessly around the room, searching for the child, questioning the truth of Maggie's words, disbelieving, even as she stared at the empty desk. "Please, no? Not Billy-Boy?"

A terrible coldness swept over her and her eyes narrowed into slits of wrath. There was no grief in her heart, no tears for the crying. She was gripped instead with a vicious anger, a fearful, raging hatred that made her want to lash out in fury, tear down every accursed stone that made Low Clough with her bare hands.

"Someone," she hissed, "will suffer for this!" and turning on her heel dismissed the carriage with a curt nod. "Someone will pay, if it takes the rest of my life!"

Her heels banged angrily on the cobbles as she strode like a creature demented towards Low Clough.

"On my mother's soul, he shall pay!"

"I tell you, Master, it's not safe in the mill! I'd be off home, if I were you. The mood's ugly, down there." Aaron Silk rubbed his shaking hands together, his ferret nose twitching. The feeling in the mill was such that it almost screamed aloud in its outrage. A child in arms could have sensed it. "They're of a mind to wreck the place, sir!"

"Over my dead body they will!" Luke growled. "And anyway 'twas an accident. The bairn slipped. Someone must have spilled oil on the floor. Find out who did it, Silk, and I'll have him fined and sacked!"

"Wouldn't do any good, Mister Holroyd. They

188

were striking for money before, but it's a matter of principle, now. A child has been killed — one of their own . . ."

"You talk as if I'd done it," Luke glowered.

"Well, sir, they're holding you responsible. They're not waiting till Saturday. They're coming out on strike right away."

Luke strode over to the window. The scene outside seemed normal enough; he could still hear the crash of the looms yet the small windows looked out with a malevolent stare and the eyes of those who crossed the yard were downcast as if they guarded a secret.

"How soon is right away?" Luke demanded.

"I don't know, Master, but *they* do. It'll only take the lifting of a finger to bring everything to a stop." He looked anxiously toward the door. "I'll have to go. I've been away from my desk for long enough. Folks'll notice . . ."

"Aye, cut along," Luke mumbled thoughtfully, "and if you hear anything else tell Dinwiddie at once."

Nasty little pest, Luke brooded as Silk sidled out. Nasty, but necessary. A mill-master must be forewarned at all times. He wished, though, that David had not taken it into his head to escort Sarah to the Manchester shops, then stay behind at the Cotton Exchange. But he'd been running Low Clough, Luke reasoned, before the lad was born. Doubtless he'd manage alone for one afternoon.

He looked down again into the mill-yard; *his*

mill-yard, *his* mill, every stick and stone of it. There had been trouble before and there'd be trouble again, but he would survive! He always had!

Sarah shut her bedroom door and refused to open it. Secretly she had been glad David was still in Manchester. She needed time alone to compose herself, control the anger that blazed white-hot inside her. By some small miracle she had been able to blot Billy-Boy from her thoughts, leaving her mind open to malice and hatred, leaving room for the bitterness there to fester and multiply.

She had decided against going to the mill and confronting her father-in-law. For once in her tempestuous life, icy logic had taken a hand and she realised she had to do nothing in anger.

It was her own fault, she acknowledged. She had let the Holroyds charm her, dull her natural antagonism. How could she, a product of the Three-streets, have been so blind? No mill-owner was to be trusted, not even David's father.

There was an ache in her throat and a pain where her heart should have been. She needed to let loose the tearing sobs that threshed inside her but the time for tears had not yet come. Later she would weep for the child.

There was a tapping on the door. "Cook's sent you a tray, madam," a small voice called. "She says you're to try to eat something."

"I don't want it," Sarah choked. "Go away and leave me alone!"

Dry-eyed, she flung herself face-down on the bed. She was lying there in the darkness, when David came home.

Gently he stroked her tumbled hair, whispered softly to her. She didn't move or answer him, yet he knew she was not asleep.

Best leave her alone tonight, he sighed. In the morning he would talk to her.

Sarah awoke to a feeling of shadowy dread, fighting wakefulness, remembering which day it was and what had to be done.

Amazingly she had slept, but sleep had not dimmed the heartache of yesterday nor dried up the tears she had scorned to cry, and the feeling of self-reproach still hung brooding over her.

She turned her head warily. Even in the curtained dimness she could see that David had not slept beside her. But that, she admitted as she tugged on the bell-pull, was all she could expect when she had pretended sleep at his approach.

"What time is it?" she asked the housemaid who drew back the curtains.

"Nearly eight o'clock, ma'am. The Master and Mr David have almost finished their breakfast," she added tactfully, holding out a silver tray. "This letter came half an hour back, by messenger."

Sarah picked up the envelope with dismay, recognising Maggie's hand, knowing before she

191

tore it open exactly what would be written there.

She read it with distaste, then crumpling it into a ball, flung it into the hearth.

When the carriage had crunched down the drive, Sarah threw back the bedclothes, then, washing and dressing quickly, ran down to the kitchen.

"I don't want anything to eat," she murmured, "but can I sit here for a while?"

"Of course you can, ma'am," Cook assured her, "but you'll do yourself no good by fretting over the child. Nothing's going to bring the poor mite back. Is it the funeral today?" she added, her plump face creased in sympathy.

"At eleven o'clock," Sarah whispered.

"Ah. Best done quickly. I suppose the parish is seeing to it?"

Sarah nodded, tight-lipped, anger sulking inside her. She wanted to lash out, make the whole of creation suffer. She marvelled that the world should go on spinning, that people could go about their daily lives as if nothing had happened.

"Billy is dead!" she wanted to scream. "And it is my fault! I should have taken him away from the workhouse, but I didn't. I should have found him a kindly home, but I couldn't spare the time!"

It would have been so easy. She had only to ask David and he'd have done it for her. But David slept alone last night, she brooded, then left for Low Clough without even wishing her goodbye.

"Mister Holroyd and Master David went early this morning," Cook supplied, breaking uncannily into Sarah's thoughts. "I took my breakfast with Mrs Parkes and she's of the opinion there'll be trouble at Low Clough before this day is out."

"I don't doubt it," Sarah acknowledged soberly. She didn't care for the stiff-backed housekeeper but she was forced to agree with her observations. Before the day was over, she pondered fearfully, the Lord only knew what might have happened.

"Try to take a cup of tea," Cook fussed, lifting the brown pot from the stove-top. "There's nothing like tea for lifting the spirits." She spooned sugar into a cup. "Come on, now," she coaxed. "Sup it up."

Obediently Sarah took it. She didn't want it but it gave her the excuse she needed to sit in the homely kitchen and bask for a little while longer in motherly concern.

"I'm going to the funeral," she announced defiantly, wincing as the steaming liquid burned her mouth. "It'll anger Mister Holroyd, I shouldn't wonder, and it won't go down well in the Three-streets either, but I'm going!"

No amount of disapproval would keep her away. It would be part of her punishment.

"Oh, Cook. It's such a heartbreak," she choked, her eyes wide with grief. "Such a terrible heartbreak . . ."

Sarah stepped down from the carriage at the

outskirts of Hollinsdyke then ordered the coachman back to High Meadow.

Can you be at the schoolroom at ten o'clock?
Maggie had written.

Head bowed, Sarah walked slowly. She had
dressed in a plain grey skirt and white blouse
tied with black ribbon. Over her head she wore
her mill-shawl, pinned beneath her chin and the
rough, familiar feel of it gave her strange comfort.

The schoolroom was silent and Maggie sat at
her desk, hands clasped, staring at the empty
desks. She jumped eagerly to her feet as Sarah
entered, gathering her into her arms.

"I'm glad you've come," she whispered. "I
thought at first there'd only be me."

"Nothing would have kept me away," Sarah
choked. "I loved that child. I tried not to, but I
did love him."

"Then that makes two of us," Maggie smiled
tearfully, "and a loving farewell is better than a
fancy funeral."

And Maggie was right, Sarah thought grimly
when they reached the undertaker's shop. There
was no pomp or display when an orphan child
was given back to the Lord. Just a handcart and
the undertaker's assistant in his second-best suit.
Three shillings and sixpence the parish allowed
for a charity burying and such a pittance did not
allow for black crêpe, or a glass-sided hearse and
mourning carriages.

Sarah touched the little coffin, reading the

words roughly printed there.

William Chapel.
Pauper.
Aged about 9 years. A.D. 1870
R.I.P.

"Rest in peace!"

She spat the words as though they were an obscenity. How dare they do this to Billy-Boy?

She drew on her breath, biting back the curses she wanted to fling at the uncaring world as she felt the grasp of Maggie's fingers on her own.

"Hush, Sarah. Stop your sorrowing. There's nothing either of us can do." Gravely she laid a posy of wild flowers on the tiny coffin.

I should have brought him some blossoms too, Sarah chided herself silently. The gardens at High Meadow were golden with daffodils, bright with flowering shrubs. She should have gathered an armful, scattered them over the miserable cart.

"Happen you're right," she choked, answering the handclasp with fingers that trembled, then, straightening her shoulders, she fell into step behind the bumping cart. Brown eyes haunted her and defenceless little hands seemed to reach out and touch her cold heart.

"William Chapel," she spoke her thoughts aloud. "He was always Billy-Boy to me. I never knew he had a name."

"Nor had he," Maggie shrugged, "but they called him William when they found him abandoned in the chapel. They're got to have something, I suppose, to write down in the register."

The cart jolted slowly through the back streets of Hollinsdyke. At every house the windows had been shuttered and women stood in small huddles, eyes downcast as they passed.

Nearing her old home Sarah's mouth ran dry and a sudden trembling took hold of her limbs. She swallowed hard on the anxiety that bubbled in her throat. The women of the Three-streets would be there. They would stand in silent judgement on her; they'd stare with dull, accusing eyes into her heart and read the shame that beat there.

Maggie sensed the heightening tension in her and pointed ahead. Still and silent, a knot of men and women waited at the top of Tinker's Row. Then as one their heads lifted and, led by a man with a black scarf knotted at his throat, fell into solemn step behind Sarah and Maggie.

Robey had come, brought them his support! Sarah let go her anxious breath. Suddenly she felt protected by his presence, uplifted by his strength.

"Walk on to Low Clough," Maggie ordered the undertaker's assistant, then seeing the alarm in Sarah's eyes whispered.

"It's all right. There'll be no bother at the mill. Robey'll see to it . . ."

Luke Holroyd stood fretting at the window of his office, hands clasped behind his back, staring down into the mill-yard.

"Something's wrong," he muttered. "I know it."

"Don't worry so, Father," David urged. "Just because Silk said the strike was to be brought forward —"

"Silk's not often wrong," Luke interrupted. "Besides, I can *feel* the trouble. It's like there's dynamite down there, ready to blow sky high any minute."

"They were supposed to have walked out yesterday and they're still working," David reasoned. "If it rested with me, I'd send Silk packing. He's a trouble-maker."

"But I'm sure he's right, for all that," the elder man defended, "and if you knew the moods of Low Clough like I know them you'd be bothered as I am!"

His head jerked upward as the small boy who had been leaning against the gates ran swiftly across the yard and disappeared through the weaving-shed doors. Almost simultaneously the mill hooter blared once, twice, three times.

Luke bit hard on his lip. There was no call for the hooter. It needed an hour, yet, to dinner-time. He raised his eyes skywards.

A cotton bale on the spinning-room hoist jerked to a standstill in its upward lift then swung suspended from side to side.

The hooter blared again and the weaving-shed doors slammed open.

"They're walking out!" Luke gasped. "And something's happening in the street!"

The funeral cart came to a stop outside Low Clough gates. Over his father's shoulder David saw the pathetic coffin and Sarah standing beside it. Her head was bravely high but her eyes were closed in pain.

"Father! It's the child!" he gasped. "It's Sarah's Billy-Boy. How could I have been so unthinking? I must go to her!"

"Nay — that you'll not!" Luke rasped. "See, the gypsy's with them and half the Three-streets too. If you go down there now you'll be begging for trouble. Go and tell Dinwiddie to send for the constabulary, if you want to do something useful. Tell him I want them here fast, but don't go down into the street if you value your health. It's not your wife's safety you have to fear for!"

His father was right, David acknowledged, but the sight of Sarah's stricken face squeezed his heart into a spasm of pain.

"Very well," he jerked. "I'll not interfere, but neither will I have the police called in. I'll not have the constabulary break up a funeral procession. Let them at least bury the child with dignity!"

"Dignity!" Luke howled. "They're not mourning! Midwinter's using the boy's death against me for his own ends, can't you see that?"

"No, I can't, sir. Tell me in all honesty. Can you swear that you and I aren't in any way to blame for that unhappy sight down there? A small boy was killed in *our* mill on one of *our* machines — machines we should have fitted with guards!"

"Now see here, David; whose side are you on?" Luke spluttered.

"I don't know, Father, but this time you're wrong about Midwinter. Maybe soon he'll use the child's death against you, but at this moment the workers need no prompting from anyone. That protest is an act of comradeship. Leave them alone! Let them mourn!"

They streamed from the weaving-shed and the spinning-room, the women carrying flowers, the men wearing armbands of mourning crêpe. One of their own had been killed and they rose as one to walk with him to his grave, parade their silent grief.

Luke stood unmoving, watching and remembering, recalling the long-ago years when he had worked in that same spinning room. Downtrodden, they'd all been but in time of direst trouble there'd been the most wonderful solidness about them. They'd stood firm against the mill-masters, caring for each other, sharing the little they had without question.

But the boot was on the other foot now and Low Clough was *his,* Luke brooded. He'd schemed to get it, worked until he was ready to drop to pay back the bankers who held it in mortgage. He was a mill-master, now. From clogs to clogs in three generations his wife had mocked, but he'd show her. He'd show his ungrateful workers too! He'd risked all he had to give them work. He'd kept Low Clough running when other masters had shut down their looms; he'd paid their wages, regular as the clock, every settling-day. Now in return they turned snarling and bit the hand that fed them! They walked out as one man in silent condemnation, gratitude forgotten!

"Very well, David," he jerked, tight-lipped. "Let them have their funeral. We'll keep the law out of it, if that's what you want!"

"I do want it, sir. I know it'll be for the best. You can't blame them for their anger, but it will die down and then we can talk, get them back to work again."

"Can we, by the heck? Can we just?" Luke growled, his mouth curving down like the jaws of a gin-trap. "We'll have to see about that!"

He stood watching as his workers filed past the little boy's coffin, silently covering the cart with their flowers. Then they formed a quiet, orderly line behind it and walked with bowed heads to the graveyard behind the parish church.

William Chapel, Pauper, would be buried there, his funeral oration intoned by the pink-cheeked curate. His coffin was shoddy, his bier mean, but no one would ever be laid to his rest with greater love than the boy who was left as a babe on the steps of Daisy Street chapel.

As the last of the procession disappeared from his view, Luke Holroyd turned sharply on his heel.

"Well now," he groaned. "We'd better see what's to be done. Have Dinwiddie come here, if you please."

The request was curt, an order no less, and David knew better than protest, even though he failed to see what help the counting-house manager might be.

When the man minced in Luke nodded gravely and indicated a chair.

Dinwiddie sniffed, hitched up his trouser creases, then sat carefully, his eyes expectant, eager to witness a fight in which he would have no active part.

"You saw what happened, Albert?" Luke demanded gravely. "You saw that charade down there?"

"That I did, Master, and downright disgraceful I call it."

"Aye. It didn't please me either, so now we must see what's to be done. I want those gates shut, Albert. I want them locked and bolted and barred! I'm closing Low Clough down. Those workers of mine walked out at their own pleasure and they'll come back at mine!"

"Eeeeeh!" Dinwiddie's chin sagged.

"Father! You can't do that," David gasped. "What you propose to do amounts virtually to a lock-out!"

"It *is* a lock-out. Low Clough is *my* mill and, if I don't choose to work it, then it's entirely *my* business!"

"But it's wrong! I'll grant you the workers

shouldn't have acted as they did, but two wrongs don't make a right!"

"Did you hear me, Albert?" Luke murmured. "Get the counting-house staff sent home, then Silk can see to things. And if I were you, lad," he jerked, turning on his son, "I'd get myself back to High Meadow and read the riot act to Sarah when she comes back!"

"Father! *Please?*"

But David's pleading fell on deaf ears. Incensed beyond measure the mill-master was intent upon revenge.

"All right," David jerked, "but I think you are making a terrible mistake, Father. And when you've realised it, don't expect *me* to dry your tears!"

Shaking with outrage he slammed from the room and the two men heard his footsteps clattering down the stairs.

"Eh, Albert, maybe the lad's right," Luke ventured. "Happen it'll do no harm to sleep on it."

"Nay, Mr Holroyd. Thy lad, if I might make so bold, knows little about the ways of a cotton-mill and nowt about mill-workers! You were t'master of Low Clough long afore he'd cut his first tooth! A lesson's what that lot need!"

"Aye, that I was," Luke ruminated, "and happen you could just be right, Dinwiddie. Happen a short sharp lesson'll not come amiss, at that!"

Dinwiddie smiled, walked sedately from the room, then closing the door behind him ran as fast as he was able in search of Aaron Silk.

Wearily Sarah slipped into High Meadow by a side door. How long she had walked after leaving Billy's graveside she couldn't tell, for the tears she longed to cry still evaded her and her heart was cold with angry grief. Now she needed to lay her torment bare, talk to David about it. David would understand. He was kind and compassionate and wouldn't deny her the solace she yearned for.

The study door was open and angry words spilled out into the hall. Without shame, she stopped to listen.

"I'll do as I think fit!" It was Luke's voice. "I'm still master here, David. *I'll* give the orders!"

"But it's insane, Father! There'll be fighting in the streets! And where are you to find enough spinners and weavers?"

"I'll find them in Manchester, lad, where spinners and weavers are begging in the streets. They'll jump at the chance of work in Low Clough. Silk'll go there on the first train tomorrow and the mill will be working again inside three days."

"But where will they live? Had you thought of that?"

"They can be quartered in the old warehouse, that's where. It's rough, but it'll mean bread in their bellies. They'll not care, if it means working again. And the Low Clough folk who walked out this morning can go hang!"

"But they didn't walk out, sir! It was only a protest. They'd have come back, if you hadn't locked the gates!"

"Nay. My mind's made up," Luke flung. "They said they could get more money at Syke Mill; let them go there."

Sarah had heard enough. Fury blazed afresh inside her. How could he do such a thing? It was mad and wicked. It was all she needed to hear. Without thought she turned and ran back the way she had come.

Luke Holroyd had gone too far this time, taken leave of his senses. Fighting in the streets, David had warned. When she told Robey what the millmaster intended. Sarah exulted, there'd be that, all right!

Jubilant, she saw no wrong in what she would do. Her father-in-law was to blame for Billy-Boy's death and now he had given her the chance to even the score. And, by God, she would make him pay!

It was late afternoon when she walked into the house in Canal Street. Her father was sitting, as he always was, in the chair by the kitchen hearth, staring fascinated into the fire.

"I'm seeking Robey," she announced without preamble. "He's not at Maggie's house and they don't know where he is. Do you?"

"No, lass, I don't," Caleb retorted. "What's your business with him?"

"Mill business," Sarah snapped. "If you see

him, tell him Luke Holroyd's closed Low Clough down."

"Tell me some news." Caleb's eyes were mocking.

"All right, then! Tell him an' all that the mill's going to be working again on Friday — with cheap labour from Manchester!"

Caleb raised his head, his eyes disbelieving.

"On your honour, girl?"

"I swear it. He's sending Aaron Silk to bring in spinners and weavers. Robey's got to be told."

"Then tell him yourself. Likely he's walking on Moor Top."

Sarah sighed impatiently, then, shaking her head at her father's disinterest, walked wearily away.

Did no one care? Now, it seemed, there was no way left but to find Robey.

She knew her wayward heart was leading her into danger. Just to think about him set her nerves twanging and voices screaming caution in her head. But she had to warn him. Billy's death had to be paid for and only Robey could help her now.

She saw him, tall against the skyline, and when she waved he stood still and watched her approach.

"If it isn't Mrs Holroyd," he called softly. "All dressed up in her mill-shawl!"

"Please," she whispered. "Don't let's fight. I'm sick to death of this awful day and I've wandered the streets till I'm weary. I came to tell you," she choked, "that Luke Holroyd is sending to Manchester for cheap labour. He's opening the mill to them, come Friday. It's true. You've got to believe me."

"I believe you," he murmured, eyes narrowing. "But why are you telling me? You're a Holroyd now. Your loyalty is to your husband."

"My loyalty is to the Three-streets, to my own people," Sarah flared. "I can't stand by and see them deprived of work, driven cap in hand to the workhouse."

"And?" he prompted.

"And there's Billy-Boy," she acknowledged reluctantly. "If there'd been guards on the machines he'd be alive now."

"So it's revenge you're looking for?"

"Aye," she admitted. "Revenge. And if you won't help me it'll make no difference. I'll not rest until —"

"Hold on now, Sarah," Robey interrupted, taking her hand in his. "Sit down and get your breath back. You look ready to drop. When did you last eat?"

"I don't know," she murmured, sinking to the cool spring grass beside him. "But hunger's nothing new to me."

"Maybe not, but driving yourself to distraction won't help."

"And sitting here won't help either. Luke Holroyd mustn't be allowed to bring in strike-breakers. There's little enough work in Hollinsdyke as

206

it is. What are you going to do about it?"

"Tonight? Nothing," he said simply. "And all we need do tomorrow is to see that Silk doesn't get on that train. It won't be too difficult to persuade him. Silk's a poor little worm. He'll see sense. And after that," he shrugged, "the mill-master must be made to see reason."

"He's a Justice of the Peace," Sarah brooded. "He's got the law on his side."

"He's got the law in his pocket, more like, but he can't fight the people. So what's really troubling you, Sarah Makin? Is it Billy-Boy at the bottom of all this?"

"Aye," she choked. "I loved him. It's my fault he's dead and I can't forgive myself. I could have taken him out of the mill, found him a kindly home, but I didn't. I was too busy playing the grand lady."

"We're all wise, with hindsight."

"But he was such a defenceless scrap, a babe, and I don't think he'd known a day's real happiness in the whole of his life," she whispered. "He was cold and hungry and most times unloved."

"You loved him, Sarah."

"But not enough, it seems. He trusted me, waited for me at the mill gates like a lost little soul. The morning he was killed I was buying satin, for a ball-gown . . ."

Her voice trembled and the long-denied tears rose again in her throat. Covering her face with hands that shook she choked:

"What will I do, Robey? His face haunts me."

"There, lass, there." Strong arms wrapped her round, held her tightly. "We're all to blame. We stand by and let them work children in the pits and mills. We're *all* guilty."

His sympathy was too much, the comfort of his arms too great. With a sob, Sarah gave way to the tears she had been unable to shed. Her grief was heart-rending and anguish arose from her throat in despairing gasps. She wept until there were no tears left to cry, until she lay spent in the cradle of his arms.

"Oh, Robey," she gasped. "You can't believe the remorse inside me."

"But I can, Sarah. I turned my back on a child too."

"*You?*"

"Aye. Emma's child. Emma was my sweetheart. We loved each other and wanted to wed. But I was proud. I wanted to give her the earth, so I left her, tramped to Liverpool and signed on a ship that was making the round-trip."

She stirred in his arms and he laid his cheek gently on hers.

"I was away at sea for nearly two years, but when we paid off I had a hundred sovereigns in my pocket. I had enough to buy a cottage and a plot of land, but —"

For a moment he didn't speak and Sarah sensed the anguish inside him, felt the slow thudding of his heart against her own. Then, with a shrugging of his shoulders, he whispered:

"When I got back home, Emma was dead and buried. She'd taken consumption and because she couldn't work there was only the workhouse to go to. I went there and they showed me the child. Emma had died, two days after it was born."

"And what became of it?"

"I looked at it with disgust, God forgive me, and left it there. It was another man's bairn, you see. She hadn't been able to wait, I thought in my anger, but it wasn't like that. Emma was a good girl. She'd been seduced by a mill-owner's son, then deserted."

"And now you hate all mill-owners?"

"Aye, that's why I go from town to town, righting wrongs, making them pay. I vowed that day I'd hold every mill-owner in creation responsible. I vowed it, over Emma's grave. I swore to make trouble for the likes of them till the day I died."

"But what brought you to Low Clough? Why Luke Holroyd's mill?"

"Nothing special. I was on my way here and I met a man. He was a cripple, with a terrible bitterness inside him. There was a score to settle, it seemed to me, so I asked him where I'd find lodging —"

"My father?"

"Aye. His cause seemed as good as any."

"And the babe?" Sarah brooded. "What became of the little one? You should have fought for *her*."

"Aye. She's the conscience inside me. I found the young buck who'd wronged Emma and thrashed him. I enjoyed doing it, Sarah, and it was worth the three months in prison it cost me. But when I was locked up I had time to think. I would take Emma's child, I decided, because that's what she'd have wanted me to do. I'd take it out of that workhouse and foster it with a good woman, pay her well for caring for it. But I was too late. When I went to claim the little thing I was shown another grave. I don't know what the bairn died of — hunger, I shouldn't wonder. Emma had called her Charity, so they told me. Now there's a name to shame a man."

He sighed, then Sarah felt the straightening of his shoulders, the tossing back of his proud head.

"So now I live on the pennies the poor drop into my begging tin and if there's no money I go hungry, like the people I try to help go hungry. It does me no harm. A man should know the feel of fire in his belly sometimes. And mill-masters will come to fear the name of Robey Midwinter."

"I'm so sorry," Sarah whispered.

"Then don't be. I don't want pity, bonny lass. Pity softens a man, makes him forget what he's sworn to do. And I'm happy enough, or was, until I met you."

"*Me?* What did I do?"

"You walked into my life one night, collecting money for Liza Nuttall's man. For one moment I thought you were Emma come back and it was like a knife twisting inside me."

"So because I looked like her you taunted me? I was alive and she was dead?"

"That's about the truth of it and, when you married young Holroyd, I tried my best to hate you."

"And you succeeded, Robey Midwinter. Two nights ago you came to High Meadow to give notice of the strike and you looked at me as if I were beneath contempt. Why did you do such a thing?"

"Because I'd found I could neither hate you nor get you out of my mind. There was no need to come to the house. I could have gone to Low Clough, I suppose, but I'd been over-long in the ale-house and there was a black mood on me. I wanted to see you with *him*, so it would help me forget you. Why did you wed him, Sarah?"

The early evening was soft, the purple twilight gentled with gold, and because it was a time of enchantment that might never come again there seemed no place on that hilltop for lies between them.

"I wed him because of you and Maggie," she whispered. "You tormented me and I tried not to care for you. But I did care. I would imagine what it would be like to sleep in your arms —"

"Maggie?" he jerked. "You thought that Maggie and me were pledged?"

"Well, aren't you? I saw you kissing one day and there was nothing genteel about it."

"I don't deny it. Maggie's a grand lass and I'm

a man — there's man's blood in my veins. Maggie is good to kiss, but there's no bond between us. How could you have been so stupid, so thoughtless?"

"Oh, I don't know." She closed her eyes wearily. "It's the way I am. There'll be no changing me."

"But didn't you realise? That night we met, you and I, here on Moor Top — we talked together amiably, yet all the time you knew that next day you'd marry David Holroyd."

"And do you remember that you picked me primroses, Robey Midwinter?" she cried, anguished. "Did you know I took them with me to the church when I wed him, pinned to my shawl?"

"No Sarah, I didn't. I'm as proud and headstrong as you are, bonny lass. But it's not too late." He gathered her closely again, whispering softly, his lips close to her cheek. "Come away with me, love."

"No, Robey! No!" She pushed him away from her, scrambling to her feet, her eyes wide with panic. "We can't be wed, you know it!"

"I'm not asking you to marry me. I'm asking you to be my woman. There's no room in my life for wedlock and I'd not be giving you riches. Life would be good, though. We'd be companions, lovers, friends. There's a fire in you that matches mine; we'd fight wrongs wherever we found them. With you beside me, Sarah lass, I could change the world!"

"Don't!" she cried. "It isn't fair. I want you so much, but my duty —"

"Duty? To a man you married in a fit of pique? Will you throw away the substance for the shadow, then, wonder for the rest of your life what it might have been like, sleeping in my arms?"

Roughly his lips found hers and longing surged through her, setting each small pulse in her body throbbing with need. She tried to think of the promises she whispered before the altar: *Keep thee only unto me.* She tried, but her mind was a surge of confused delight and her body so limp with longing that she was forced to cling desperately to him.

"No!" she moaned. "No, Robey!"

But even as her lips denied him her heart shouted with joy.

"Sarah, sweetheart." His voice was soft in her ear, his arms strong and sure about her. "I need you so much."

She closed her eyes in silent submission as they slipped gently to the grass at their feet and the scent of the earth lulled her senses like wine.

Above them, dipping and drifting in the darkening sky, a curlew called softly, but they did not hear it.

The sky was indigo velvet and the first star of evening low in the sky. Fingers entwined, shoulders touching, they lay bemused and shy, reluctant to speak lest the magic be lost.

It was Robey who pulled them gently back to earth. Gathering her into his arms again he whispered:

"You can't leave me now, Sarah. When my work here is finished, say you'll come with me."

"I don't know. I can't think, darling. David is my husband and I owe him —"

It seemed wrong, at that moment, even to speak his name and guilt flushed her cheeks.

"You owe him *nothing*, Sarah. You belong to me, now."

"I'm married to David," she insisted dully.

"And it's me you love!" he exulted. "I won't let us be parted."

"Don't, Robey. Give me time to think things out," she pleaded. 'If you press me now I shall say yes and that wouldn't be right. I've done so many foolish things in the past, rushed head-down at life without a thought. This time there must be no mistakes. I must be sure."

"Maybe you're right," he conceded reluctantly, "but it'll not stop me wanting you."

She smiled into the darkness, then, kissing the tip of her forefinger, laid it gently to his lips.

"Hush now. Don't spoil this loveliness. We've so much to be thankful for, you and me. We're young and alive, Robey, yet down there, in that awful town, there are people who are old and sick and hungry." She raised herself on her elbow and looked out into the dark distance, over to the hollow below them where Hollinsdyke lay. "There's a little boy who —"

She stopped suddenly, eyes narrowed, and tugged at his arm.

"Look! Down there!"

Smoke billowed upward, illuminated in a fierce red glow, and great tongues of flame licked at the sky.

"Something's ablaze!" he gasped, struggling to his feet. "It's big — like a mill — though which one it is I can't tell."

But Sarah knew. To the left of the fire the spire of the parish church stood black against the glow and to the north the tall towers of the Town Hall were clear to see. There was no doubting the position of the blazing mill.

"It's Low Clough!" she gasped. "It's burning from end to end!"

Nine

There could be no doubting it. The mill Sarah had cursed so passionately was ablaze.

"Hurry," Robey jerked, grasping her hand. "I must go. They'll need help."

Picking their way, slipping and sliding on the rough path they stumbled through the darkness to the road that led to Hollinsdyke.

"How could it have happened?" Sarah panted.

"Cotton dust exploding, I shouldn't wonder," Robey flung, over his shoulder, "or maybe a gas-jet . . ."

He peered ahead, muttering under his breath as the gravel beneath his feet shifted, sending him skidding downward at a giddy run.

Briars reached out along their path, tearing Sarah's skirts, clawing at her ankles, but she blundered after him, refusing to cry out, knowing there was worse to come, that this was only the start of the nightmare.

There'll be trouble at Low Clough before this day is out.

The words beat inside her brain as the sombre prophesy began to turn into stark reality. But how had it happened? Mill fires were commonplace and usually put out quickly. Mill-workers were experienced fire-fighters, quick to preserve their livelihood, knowing only too well that a burned-out mill was of use to no one.

But Low Clough had been idle, its workers shut out by Luke's anger, so how, Sarah fretted, had the fire begun?

Robey left her at the end of Clough Street. "Stay here," he commanded. "Yonder's no place for a woman." He looked at her thougtfully, then said, "This changes nothing. I still want you."

"I know," she whispered. "But give me time."

"I'll grant you that," he nodded soberly, "but I'll not wait forever for an answer."

Trembling, she watched him go, trying to find comfort in the remembered joy of their coupling, but she was cold with shock and an indefinable fear seemed to have taken hold of her senses.

A fire-cart clattered past, bell clanging, the horses straining beneath the cracking whip, and she cowered for shelter into a doorway.

This is my doing, she thought, panic rising unchecked in her throat. I called down misfortune on Low Clough, ill-wished Luke Holroyd. I am to blame.

Drawn by morbid fascination, she walked toward the mill, eyes round with horror. Flames licked from every window like ghoulish tongues and a snapping filled the air as the roof timbers blazed frenziedly. Silhouetted against the glow, men and women toiled in a chain, passing along buckets of water, and she recognised them as Low Clough workers, the spinners and weavers

Luke Holroyd had locked out.

Wide-eyed she stood, trying to gather in her thoughts but her muddled mind refused to accept reality. It was as if she had stepped from heaven into hell, as if her new-found love was a dream and she had been awakened from it roughly to stare into a nightmare.

Why did she crave vengeance? She had watched the earth receive the tiny coffin and vowed that Billy-Boy's death should not go unpunished. Why hadn't she realised that a graveside oath was the most binding of pledges?

"Heaven help me, I'm a wicked creature," she whispered. "I meant it, Lord. I was angry because I blamed myself for Billy's death and I wanted revenge. But not this; never this."

"Sarah!" Hands grasped her shoulders roughly. "Where have you been? I've been out of my mind with worry!"

David wiped a sleeve across his face, anger mingling with relief. His shirt was torn, his clothes drenched. Smoke had blackened his face and his soft pale hair, making it hard to distinguish him from the roughly dressed men around them.

"You've been gone all day. I've had people searching the streets for you!"

"You might have known where I was," Sarah whispered dully, unwilling to meet his eyes lest he should see her betrayal there. "I went to Billy's funeral."

"I know," he gasped impatiently. "But that was hours ago."

"Oh, leave me be," she choked. "I was upset. I couldn't think straight. I just walked and walked, I suppose."

And found comfort in another man's arms, her conscience reminded.

"Dearest, I'm sorry." Anxiety giving way to relief he gathered her to him. "You're back safely now and that's all I care about. The carriage is standing by in Water Street. Go home. I'd feel better if you did."

"I'm staying," she jerked stubbornly, shrugging away his arms. "There must be something I can do to help."

"Then, if you must, go to my father. Try to keep him out of harm's way. He's badly shocked."

"Yes, he would be," she murmured, her face wooden. "He loves that mill, doesn't he, like it was his child?"

"Oh my dear, forgive me." Quick to recognise the rebuke, David's voice was instantly contrite. "I should have realised how much Billy-Boy meant to you. I should have been with you. I'm so sorry."

"Oh, stop saying you're sorry!" she gasped. "It's over now. Leave it. Let the child rest."

She drew her shawl around her, unable to look into his face, and turning abruptly she left him, her back stiff with defiance. She wished she could hate him as she hated his father. She wanted Robey, and David stood between them, yet she felt only pity for him and anger against herself for being so weak as to care that she had wronged him.

Luke was standing alone by the mill gates when Sarah found him.

"Come away, Master," she demanded, tugging at his sleeve. "You're much too near. If anything should fall —"

But he stood his ground as though he needed to be near his mill until the end.

"Eh, lass," he choked. "This is a terrible night." He turned to face her and she was shocked to see that his cheeks were wet with tears. "Who could have done such a thing?"

"Done?" Sarah hissed. "You mean it wasn't an accident?"

"No, by heaven, it wasn't!" he ground. "How could it be? The mill wasn't working. That fire broke out in four different places. 'Twas deliberate!"

He closed his eyes as if the sight was too much to bear, as though he were standing helpless, watching the dying of a beloved mistress.

Scattered over the pavement lay the mill books and ledgers and the solemn-faced clock from the wall of his office, carried out of the counting-house while there had yet been time, and beside them Dinwiddie stood trembling, his bowler hat askew, a black tin cash-box clutched in his arms.

"Deliberate?" Sarah demanded, the uneasiness inside her refusing to be ignored. "What proof is there?"

"I can *feel* it," Luke ground. "That's proof enough for me. Besides, there's someone in there." He nodded grimly toward the mill. "He's been seen by a fireman and Silk caught sight of him too."

"Silk'd tell you black was white," Sarah flung, "and you'd believe him!"

But even as she spoke her eyes followed Luke's pointing finger and she knew then why she had been so afraid.

"See?" he demanded triumphantly. "On the top floor? Didn't I tell you?"

She had seen him, stark against the flames, his head thrown back defiantly, his twisted limbs grotesque against a backcloth of fire, and though she could not hear him she knew he was laughing.

"Father!" she cried, her voice a whimper of disbelief.

The ground beneath her feet tilted and her head spun so that she had to grasp Luke's arm to prevent herself sinking into the blackness that swirled around her. But she did not fall fainting at his feet, for through the blackness came the memory of Caleb Makin's bitterness.

'Luke Holroyd is going to get his comeuppance and I want to live long enough to see it. I want to stand there, and laugh!'

Words her father had used hit her like a whiplash, shocking her into instant alertness.

'I'd give anything to see this filth about me burning.'

She forced her eyes upward again, praying that what she had seen was unreal, a frightening apparition born of her guilt-ridden conscience.

But Caleb was no ghost. A flesh and blood man stood at a top-storey window, calling down defiance, contemptuous of the danger around him.

"It's Caleb!" Luke gasped. "What's he up to? If he doesn't shift himself there'll be no way out!" He cupped his hands to his mouth. "Caleb Makin! Come down, man, before it's too late!"

Sarah closed her eyes, willing her father to safety, directing him with her mind to the gantry-like bridge that connected the mill to the counting-house. The fire hadn't reached there yet. Hadn't he the sense to save himself?

But a madman knows no sense and her father was mad. He'd been mad for years, locked away in his own little hell. She had known it and chosen to ignore it.

"Caleb! I'm coming in!" Dashing across the yard, ignoring the cries of warning, Luke ran headlong into the blazing building. "Hold on, Caleb, old friend. I'll get you out!"

"Go after him," Sarah pleaded as he disappeared through the weaving-shed doors. "He'll be killed! Won't someone *do* something?" Blindly she ran forward. "Father-in-law, come back!"

Dimly above the noise she heard her husband's voice.

"Sarah! Sarah, look out!" and she felt herself being thrown violently off balance to fall, arms

flailing to the ground.

In that instant the mill roof crashed in, sending up a cascade of sparks, setting free the pent-up fire to roar flaming into the sky.

"The wall! It's going!" a voice cried. *"Run!"*

Urged by the instinct to survive, fear pumping strength into her limbs, Sarah flung herself forward, scrambling blindly on hands and knees away from the danger. A pain shot through her head, agonizing in its intensity, and red flashes forked before her eyes.

With a gasp, she fell insensible.

She was sitting on the pavement when she came to, with Dinwiddie bending over her anxiously rubbing her hands.

"What happened?" she mumbled, pain crashing through her head.

"Eh, how you weren't killed I'll never know!"

"Something hit me," she whispered, wanting to close her eyes again, drift back into the cushioning blackness.

"Aye, a piece of rubble. The side wall caved in and you'd have been under it if it hadn't been for Mister David. He pushed you out of the way."

"David?" Sarah choked, dry-mouthed. "Where is he?"

She struggled to her feet then swayed as the ground beneath her tilted.

"Where is he?" she demanded.

"Over yonder," Dinwiddie nodded grimly. "He was hit by a lump of falling stone. The doctor's with him. It's his head, they say. Hurt bad, I reckon."

This is a nightmare, Sarah thought wildly. A living, seeing nightmare. She felt the urge to laugh and laugh, but tears were coursing down her cheeks.

"Mrs Holroyd," Dinwiddie urged, shaking her arm, "Let me help you to the carriage."

"No! I must stay here." She would be all right, really she would, if only the weeping would stop. "Just give me a minute." Gulping hard on her tears she choked:

"Send someone to High Meadow, Mr Dinwiddie. Tell them what has happened and ask Mrs Parkes to have a bed ready and clean strips of linen. And hot water — plenty of it!"

Then she ran to her husband's side, fearful of what she might find, her throat tight with apprehension.

David lay unmoving, his clothes wet and muddy, his face ashen beneath the grime. The man beside him nodded, then rose to his feet.

"I am Doctor Harcourt, ma'am." He raised his hat briefly. "I fear your husband is unconscious," he murmured. "How long it will be before he recovers I cannot tell. There are no visible signs of injury, a fact which disturbs me, for it may be that the contusions are internal. If that is so, there is very little we can do."

Sarah gazed with horror at the still form. David had saved her life, perhaps at the expense of his own. He loved her and she had betrayed him.

"Let him be all right," she prayed desperately. "And Caleb my father, and Luke — please get them out safely."

She looked again at the blazing mill, at the mill-yard, choked with smouldering rubble, at the man who lay still as death at her feet and realised she had just asked for a miracle. And miracles never happened, she thought dully. Especially in God-forsaken Hollinsdyke.

"Doctor Harcourt," she breathed. "I don't want my husband to go to the infirmary. I want him nursed at home."

"You have chosen wisely," the doctor nodded, "and I will come with you, see him comfortably settled."

"Thank you sir," she whispered gratefully, hugging her shawl around her trembling body, knowing that if she lived for a hundred years more she would never forget this night.

It was then she saw Robey, pushing his way toward her. He was stripped to the waist, his body gleaming with sweat.

"Sarah! They told me you'd been hurt!"

"No. I'm all right." She nodded toward the improvised stretcher. "David took the brunt of it. The doctor is worried about him."

She lifted her eyes to his, silently begging him not to make demands, and he read her thoughts as though she were a part of him.

"Don't fret, bonny lass. Go where your duty lies," he said gently.

She nodded, unable to answer him for the guilt

and love that fought within her.

"Will I have Maggie come to you?" he asked.

"No. I'll be all right." She needed time to think, sort out her thoughts, arrange things in their proper order. Best she should be alone. "I must go now. David is in need of me."

She stopped, looking over his shoulder to the police constables who pointed in their direction. She knew at once that something was wrong. She could see it in the set of their faces, their slow, sure walk.

"Are you looking for me?" she demanded, fear icing through her. "Who sent for you?"

"You'll be young Mrs Holroyd?" the elder of the three remarked, touching his hat in a brief salute. On his arm he wore the rank of sergeant and a polished wooden truncheon swung aggressively from his jutting fingertip. "It was Mr Luke Holroyd sent for us, ma'am, and not without good cause, it would seem!" Then turning to Robey he demanded, "Are you Robey Midwinter, and do you lodge at Dan Ormerod's house, in Albert Court?"

"Aye."

"Then can you tell me where you were tonight between half-past seven and nine o'clock?"

"I can," he retorted, his eyes narrowing as the men inched menacingly closer. "But I won't!"

"Then I must warn you, Midwinter, that you are suspected of maliciously causing the fire at this mill and tell you that you are not obliged to answer my questions." The words were spoken clearly and carefully, their implication unmistakable. "But, if you can satisfy me that you were seen to be elsewhere at that time, then you have nothing to fear."

"I was nowhere near the mill. I was walking," Robey asserted. "I was on Moor Top hill."

"And is there someone who saw you?"

"There isn't, but I *was* there."

"Robey!" Sarah gasped as the implication of the questioning became clear. "That's not true! You were —"

"I was alone," harshly he cut her short. *"Alone."*

"But someone can prove you were there. Tell them," she pleaded.

The sergeant shrugged. He would get nothing from Midwinter, but the woman was a different matter. Young Mrs Holroyd knew something. Her frightened eyes gave her away and the agitation in her face. She'd be the one to tell them.

"Well now, ma'am? Can you throw any light on this matter?" He spoke softly, suggestively. *"Could* someone have seen him on Moor Top hill?"

"No one saw me!" Robey spat. "I was alone but I *was* there and it's up to you to prove different!" Then, rounding on Sarah, holding her eyes with his own, he hissed, "Say nothing, do you hear? *Nothing.*"

"Well, Mrs Holroyd?" the sergeant pressed. "Is there something we should know?"

"There's nothing," Robey flung, his voice angry. "Leave her alone, I tell you!"

"As you wish," the policeman shrugged, "but you leave me no choice. Robey Midwinter, I am arresting you on suspicion of wilfully causing the firing of Low Clough mill and warn you again that you have the right in law to remain silent."

With practised alacrity the constables seized his arms, jerking them behind his back, clicking handcuffs on his wrists.

"Robey!" Sarah gasped. "Tell them!"

The sergeant hesitated, raising a questioning eyebrow, but the man they called the gypsy threw back his head, laughing.

"Tell them what? There's nothing to tell, Mrs Holroyd. Go home. Take care of your husband and leave me to look after myself."

With that he turned on his heel, a constable on each arm and strode defiantly away.

"Sergeant," Sarah gasped. "Why are you doing this? What right have you to handcuff him? What is he to be charged with?"

"It could be arson, ma'am."

"But that's a serious offence. How can you be sure he did it?"

"I'm as sure as I can be, Mrs Holroyd. And I said it *could* be arson he's charged with. It might be worse. Much worse!"

But Robey hadn't set fire to Low Clough, she thought wildly. He couldn't have. 'Say nothing!' he'd commanded. But there could be worse to come, the sergeant had said and, if that were so, how would it be possible to remain silent?

"We are ready, ma'am." A hand grasped her arm and the doctor's precise voice rasped into her thoughts. "We must make haste . . ."

"I'm coming," she whispered, her voice strange-sounding in her ears. "I'm coming."

She stumbled after him in a daze. The world had gone mad. Completely mad.

Mrs Parkes was waiting at the front door of High Meadow as the carriage drew to a gentle halt. Behind her, her plump face creased with anxiety, Cook nodded her sympathy.

"Everything is in order, ma'am," the house-keeper murmured, directing the men who carried David's still body into the house. "And I took the liberty of sending a telegraph message to Mrs Luke, in Cumberland."

"Thank you," Sarah breathed, hurrying up-stairs behind the doctor. Oh, but it would be good to have Charlotte back, to hand over all responsibility then find a small, dark corner in which to hide herself away from the frightening world.

"Cook and I will stay close at hand." The housekeeper's voice was firm and reassuring and Sarah wondered why she could have ever imag-ined her to be cold and aloof.

The clock ticked slowly, loudly, emphasising Sarah's aloneness, sending apprehension cours-ing through her. She wondered what fresh misery the night could unfold and if she would be strong enough to bear it. She was still reeling from the blow the doctor had delivered, just before he left.

"I'm afraid I must leave you alone," he had said, his fingertips measuring the pulse at David's wrist, "but I shall call again at first light. And of course you must send for me at once, if there is any change."

Mutely Sarah nodded.

"At no time must the patient be left. He must be watched constantly."

"I understand," Sarah whispered. "How long might it be before he awakens?"

"That I cannot tell. I've known similar cases to be many days before improving." He fingered his beard, his face grim. "I am afraid you must accept the fact, distressing though it is, ma'am, that your husband could sink into a coma from which there will be no awakening." For the first time that evening he looked at her kindly, his eyes softening. "And now, will you compose yourself, my dear, for I fear I have news to impart that can only add to your burdens."

Sarah rose to her feet, her eyes wide with panic. What more could happen? What new madness was to come? But in her heart she already knew.

"It's my father, isn't it?"

"I'm sorry. It happened when the roof collapsed. The police sergeant wanted to tell you, but I forbade it. I undertook to break the sad news myself, when you had had time to adjust to your husband's injuries."

"And David's father?" she choked, stiff-lipped.

"Mr Holroyd is dead too. They were brought out and laid in the counting-house."

"Dear heaven —"

'*Worse to come,*' the sergeant had said.

Sarah hid her face in her hands, closing her eyes tightly, shutting out the horror. If she wasn't so numb, she thought, she could scream and scream until she awoke from this dreadful nightmare.

Perhaps she too was going mad? Perhaps it was all in her mind? But her mud-covered clothes were real and her sodden shoes and the smell of the fire on her hands.

She opened her mouth and let out a piercing scream and in that instant she seemed to hear Charlotte's voice, sharp with rebuke.

"*Stop it at once. Pull yourself together!*"

As if she had been slapped, her cry ended in a moan.

"I'm sorry," she choked, her body shaking with pent-up sobs. "Forgive me."

"Of course, ma'am. Of course." He patted her arm awkwardly. "Let me ring for a sip of brandy and perhaps someone to sit with you."

"No sir, I thank you," her voice was low, but firm. "I would like to be alone to compose myself. And if I need help I have only to ring."

"Then, if you are sure, I must leave you," he said reluctantly. "There are things I must see to, at the mill."

"I am quite sure, and thank you, Doctor Harcourt, for your help. You have been very kind."

She had nodded a goodbye, straightening her back and lifting her chin as Charlotte would have done. And until Charlotte returned, she realised, she had to shoulder all responsibility herself.

The hours passed slowly. She was living. Sarah thought, through the longest, the most terrifying hours of her life.

She looked dully at her husband's inert body. His hands in hers were cold, his breathing shallow, and he lay without even the smallest sigh escaping his lips or the briefest flickering of an eyelid.

A gentle tapping on the door caused her to spring to her feet, grateful for the nearness of another soul.

"Miss Ormerod's come, ma'am," the wide-eyed housemaid whispered. "Will you see her?"

"Of course," Sarah nodded. "But what time is it?"

"It's morning. Gone eight o'clock."

A new day; a new beginning. Sarah longed to throw back the curtains, let in the sunlight, but this was now a house of mourning and had to remain deeply shrouded until the dead had been laid to rest.

"Show Miss Ormerod into the small sitting-room, then ask Mrs Parkes if she will sit beside Mr David's bed," she asked, her body limp with gratitude that Maggie had come.

The school-teacher was standing by the fireside

her face warm with sympathy. She held out her arms and Sarah flew into them like a child in need of comfort.

"There, there," Maggie soothed. "It's all right. Nothing more can happen now."

"But it's all so awful — a bad dream. And it's so lonely in this great house — so dark and still."

"Things are always worse before they get better," Maggie smiled gently. "I've come to say how sorry I am about — well, about everything, and to let you know that if you need me . . . ?"

Sarah nodded gratefully. "Bless you," she choked.

"And how is your husband, Sarah? It was a brave thing he did."

"Yes. I owe him my life. But there's no change. He just lies there. Oh, I need so much to talk to someone, Maggie."

"Aye, there's things to be said on both sides," Maggie nodded. "Happen this isn't the right time, but they'll have to be talked about, sooner or later. You know what I mean?"

"I think so. I think the police will come to see me before very long and I've got to have things sorted out in my mind before they do. But I'm so weary," she sighed, "I can't think properly."

"Then let's take it gently, put first things first, shall we, Sarah? Happen then we'll find we're both bothered about the same things."

Not until they were settled comfortably before the fire did Sarah say:

"You want to talk about my father?"

"I do. I'm right sad he's gone, but he was a sick man, Sarah, and most times in pain. He's at peace now and it's the living we've got to care about. It wasn't Robey set fire to Low Clough. I know you are burdened with trouble, but it's got to be said. They've arrested an innocent man and I think you know it!"

"What do you mean?" Sarah gasped. "Why should I know it? Who have you been talking to?"

"To Robey," Maggie acknowledged quietly. "They let me see him this morning at first light."

"And he *told* you? He told you that — ?"

"He told me nothing, save that he didn't do it. But I know he didn't. It was your father, wasn't it, Sarah?"

"What makes you so sure — about my father, I mean?" Relief washed over Sarah. "Who's been talking?"

"Only your father. He told me, you see — as near as makes no matter — that he was going to do it. Billy-Boy's death upset him badly, brought back his own injuries. He said you'd told him that Luke Holroyd was bringing in cheap labour and I think that was the last straw."

"Yes, I told him that, I admit it, but he didn't seem much put out, at the time."

"He was, though. Underneath he was mad with rage. He came to Albert Court, asking for Robey, muttering about Low Clough. 'That cursed mill,' he was saying. 'One day someone's going to burn it to the ground.' I was worried about him. I told

234

him to go home then went out to try to find Robey. It wasn't any use, though. He could have been anywhere."

"Aye, he could have been," Sarah admitted, low-voiced, "and you're right, Maggie. Hard though it is to admit it, I know my father was to blame. But I'd hoped Robey could convince the police he'd had nothing to do with the fire. I'd hoped to keep my father's name out of it, but it'll all have to come out, I suppose," she shrugged.

"And you think that'll be the end of it and everything will be all right? You think the police are going to believe you?" Maggie whispered. "Oh, no! They want it so that justice can be seen to be done. Robey has caused them a lot of bother of late and this is the chance they've been hoping for. They'll say he's trying to lay the blame on a man who can't defend himself."

"But my father was there, in the mill."

"They'll say he was a madman, Sarah; they'll say he just got himself trapped there . . ."

"Then what's to be done?" A small pulse of fear beat at Sarah's throat. "How can we convince them?"

"I don't know. I asked Robey outright where he was last night, but he wouldn't say. He's hiding something, but I'll find out what it is, I swear it!"

Sarah sat unspeaking, staring into the flames. Maggie was right. The police would never accept that her father had caused the fire. They would want a living scapegoat, not a dead one. She alone could prove Robey's innocence, but, in doing so, she would condemn herself for the wanton she had become.

But would it matter? Soon she had to come to a decision. She had to choose between the man who loved her and the man who held her bewitched. Maybe, if things were brought into the open, that decision would be made for her.

But not just yet. She had taken all she could, and besides, there was David to think about. How could she hurt him so?

"I must go to my husband," she jerked, rising abruptly to her feet. "He could awaken at any moment and I want to be there. Can I order the carriage for you, Maggie? It's a long step back to Hollinsdyke."

"No, I thank you. Think of the talk in the Three-streets," Maggie smiled, pulling on her gloves. "And the walk will do me good. I've a lot of thinking to do. Someone in Hollinsdyke knows where Robey was last night, someone who must come forward and prove he couldn't have fired the mill. She's got to be found."

"She?"

"Of course. It's got to be a woman," Maggie flung tersely. "Why else would he be so cussed stupid, will you tell me? But I'll find her. I'll not rest, until I do! I'll leave no stone unturned —"

"Oh, why can't you leave it?" Sarah gasped, "Don't you know that when you start turning stones all sorts of nasty things can crawl from under them? And what is it to you, Maggie? Why are you doing all this?"

"Don't you know? Hadn't you realised how much Robey means to me? I've loved him since he first set foot in Hollinsdyke. Oh, he'll never love me," she whispered, her eyes wistful. "No woman will ever completely own his heart. But I'd be glad to accept what he was willing to give. I'd go with him, if he asked me, to the back of beyond." She looked up, smiling softly. "There now, I've said it. Tell me I'm a fool, Sarah."

"No, I'll not do that. But go easy, dear friend. Don't get hurt."

"I'll try not, but there's nothing so foolish on the face of this earth as a woman in love," Maggie sighed, gathering Sarah to her, kissing her goodbye. "And I'll come again soon. Try not to worry too much."

Sarah stood in the doorway, watching until Maggie's small, determined figure had rounded the bend in the drive, then, sighing, she closed the heavy doors and walked reluctantly upstairs.

Maggie was right. No one would ever get inside his heart, she conceded. No woman would wholly own him. Not even Emma or the chance-child called Charity who was his conscience.

No one will ever possess Robey Midwinter, she thought, but I at least know what it is to lie in his arms. So look if you must, Maggie, for the woman who can free him. You'll not find her — not until she chooses to be found. And when that time comes the whole of Hollinsdyke will know who she is, because happen she'll walk out of town at his side!

Slowly she opened the bedroom door and, nodding to the woman who kept vigil there, took her place at the bedside again.

"He didn't move, Mrs Parkes? There's been no sign of — ?"

"No, ma'am, I'm sorry," came the gentle reply. "But take comfort. Mr David is very dear to us all and we are praying hard for him," she whispered, closing the door quietly behind her.

'And he is dear to me too,' Sarah's heart sighed. 'He is a good, kind man who loves me truly and it is because of that love that he lies here now, a step away from death. If I could, I would love him as he deserves to be loved, but my stupid heart won't let me. Soon I must make a choice and it will be the most heart-breaking thing I will ever have to do . . .'

Taking the cold, still hand in her own, Sarah held it to her cheek.

"Oh, David," she whispered, "I have made such a mess of it all. No matter what decision I come to, someone I care for will be hurt . . ."

Ten

The afternoon slipped slowly by and still David lay unmoving in the darkened room. At his side Sarah sat thinking of her father's wasted life, remembering him as he once had been, his mind and body whole. Better she should think of him that way than the bitter, twisted man he had become; better by far she should grieve for the handsome, laughing man who died, really, the day the Low Clough machine mangled his body. And from that time on loathing had festered inside Caleb until it finally destroyed him. And yet, Sarah thought sadly, Luke Holroyd had plunged without thought into the blazing mill.

I was taught to hate him, Sarah pondered. I blamed him for Billy-Boy's death, yet he died for my father without thought for himself.

Now they lay side by side; the crippled spinner and the mill-master, equal in death. Now David lay sick, his life in Fate's inconstant hands, and Robey had been wrongfully imprisoned. And all, she admitted wearily, because I was determined to have revenge, because there is a wilful streak in me that has been my undoing.

If only she was not so tired, so numb. If only Charlotte would return, take the load from her weary shoulders. If only —

"If only I had once stopped to think," she

whispered to the impartial room, as a tear ran down her cheek.

Charlotte came home to High Meadow in the early evening, alighting from the hansom-cab with her customary aplomb. Dressed in black, widow's weeds floating behind her, she was in complete control of her every movement. Not even death, Sarah thought, peering through the bedroom curtains, could catch her mother-in-law unawares.

Relief washing over her, she ran to the banister, leaning over. Never had she thought to see the day she would be grateful for Charlotte's presence, yet here she was, weak with relief, almost smiling a welcome.

"My dear," Charlotte sailed up the stairs. "This is a sad homecoming." She held Sarah at arm's length. "Heaven preserve us, girl, you look dreadful! When did you last sleep?"

Without waiting for an answer she hurried into the sickroom.

"How long has he been like this?" she whispered, the mask slipping from her face as she looked sadly at her son.

"Since last night. The doctor is very worried."

"Doctor Harcourt," Charlotte jerked, "is an old fool! My son has a robust constitution; of course he'll get well. He must," she ended in a whisper.

Sarah reached for the older woman's hand, pressing it reassuringly. "I'm so sorry," she whispered, "about everything. Mr Holroyd was a very brave man. He tried to save my father."

"Sorry?" Charlotte smiled wryly. "Ah, yes. We all have much to be sorry for, but it's too late now, for regrets. I spent my life hating every minute I was married to Luke. If only I'd put as much effort into trying to care for him a little more."

Peeling off her gloves, unpinning her bonnet, she sank sighing into the chair at her son's bedside.

"How did it happen?" she demanded brusquely.

"It was my fault," Sarah breathed. "David pushed me out of harm's way when the wall fell and got hurt doing it. Don't be angry with me."

"No one is going to be angry," Charlotte replied, "and it's plain to see you've had more than enough to contend with. Parkes shall sit with David while I interview the undertaker and you, my gel, shall be put to bed with a laudanum draught. You look as if you haven't slept for days!"

"It seems as if I haven't," Sarah choked. "I don't think I shall ever sleep easy again. I shall always blame myself."

"Tut, girl, there's no putting back the clock. Just oblige me by taking yourself off to bed!"

It was good to be bullied so, Sarah thought drowsily as she lay back against the pillows. She wanted to sleep and sleep and when she awakened she wanted to see David's head on the pillow beside her, know that her greatest worry was the choosing of material for a ball-gown, that Billy-Boy would be there, waiting for his soup, and that Low Clough was as it had always been.

Yet to wish that would be to banish the loving she had shared on the twilight hilltop and that she could never do. That loving was real and because of it she was faced with an agonising choice. David was kind and good and loved her as she didn't deserve to be loved. David had put his life at risk for her sake. And Robey promised her nothing but hardship and a heart that could never be wholly hers. But he could turn her bones to ice and her blood to fire and last night, when she lay in his arms, she had reached up and touched the stars . . .

Sarah awoke reluctantly, wanting to sleep longer but knowing she had not to, instinct directing her thoughts to the sickroom. Pulling on a robe she swayed unsteadily, for the laudanum still held her bemused.

"Thank heaven you've come, child!" Charlotte jumped to her feet as Sarah pushed open the door. "He's coming round, I'm sure of it. His eyes moved."

Sarah stood motionless, watching her husband's still face as Charlotte moistened his lips with water. His breathing was more regular, she conceded, but, that apart, she could see no change in his condition. Was her mother-in-law seeing only what she wanted to see?

"Are you sure?"

"Of course I'm sure. He *will* get well." For a moment Charlotte gazed tenderly at her son, then taking a deep, steadying breath, said quietly:

"Sit down, Sarah. You and I must talk. I want you to know that when David brought you here I was deeply angry. But you are married now and I realise I must do all I can to help."

"Please?" Sarah begged uneasily. "Can't we leave it? Can't we talk later?"

"No. I am determined to have my say, so please listen. Whilst I have been sitting here, Sarah, I have had time to think and I know it will be best, when David is well, for me to leave High Meadow."

"But, ma'am, there's no need —"

"There is every need. There cannot be two mistresses in one house no matter how big it is and besides I want to go. I came here unwillingly as a bride and I have known little happiness in this place." She sighed, her voice unsteady with emotion. "The fault was mine. Luke needed to be loved and I refused him. I should have tried harder, Sarah, as you must try."

Sarah lowered her head, her agitated fingers plucking at the edge of the counterpane, her heart thudding heavily.

"I think in time you and David will find happiness together," Charlotte urged softly, "and when your children come there'll be noise and turmoil in this mausoleum and I shall visit from time to time and spoil them dreadfully."

"But where will you go?" Sarah whispered.

"There are plenty of places, I suppose," the older woman shrugged. "Luke settled money on me when we married. I have hardly touched it. Perhaps I shall buy a small house in London. I'm not sure yet. I only know that you and David must be left alone together."

"Please don't say any more!" Sarah pleaded, guilt surging through her. "Don't make plans. It tempts Fate."

"Maybe," Charlotte smiled ruefully. "Maybe not. I only know I shall not stay in Hollinsdyke. This is David's house now and it will be up to you, Sarah, to do what I never did. You must make it into a *home*. You will give the orders, from now on. You are the mistress of Luke's Folly now," she whispered bitterly. "I bequeath it to you gladly."

"And if I don't want it?" Sarah gasped. "If I don't want to be mistress, give orders?"

"Then you must learn. It's not only High Meadow. You have the people of Hollinsdyke to think about. You have no choice."

But she *had* a choice, Sarah thought wildly. Robey wanted her. Soon he would come and she would have to give him her answer. She would have to choose between love and duty, poverty or riches. Her loyalty lay with David, her heart with Robey.

She closed her eyes. *Please, Lord, help me . . .*

Then her head jerked up and she drew in her breath.

"There!" Charlotte cried. "David moved. You saw it too, didn't you? Oh, pray for him, Sarah! Pray as you've never prayed before! Make a bargain with the Almighty," she urged desperately. "Promise Him that if David recovers you will try to be a loving wife, that you will learn to care for your husband."

"But I do care," Sarah cried, sadly. "I have never shirked my wifely duties."

"Duties? Is love a duty, then?"

Mutely Sarah dropped her gaze, unable to look into her mother-in-law's eyes.

"I know you didn't care for my son when you married him. I could read it in your eyes," Charlotte pressed. "But I know he is very much in love with you. Won't you try, Sarah, as I should have tried?"

Wide-eyed, panic taking her limbs and shaking them mercilessly, Sarah looked at her husband. She felt like a small, trapped animal. Had she to make it, that bargain with God? Had she to promise, then, that in return for David's recovery she would remain his wife? Was it her destiny to stay in Hollinsdyke or should she follow Robey, help him right wrongs, fight for lost causes? Charity, they said, began at home, but was she brave enough to try to forget the wildness that flamed through her at Robey's touch? Was it really true that blazing passion flamed hot and died quickly? Did Robey love her as she loved him?

David loved her. David had been prepared to die for her, she conceded soberly. She owed him her life and now he was fighting for his own. Did she have a choice?

Hesitating no longer, she took his hands in her own and silently began to pray.

Please, Lord, help him. Let him awaken soon and be well. He's a good man and if you'll give him back, I'll stay with him, be a good wife. I'll try to love him as he loves me. I swear it Lord, on Billy-Boy's soul . . .

Then weakly she began to cry and her tears were for a love that was over, for a moment of passion that had to fade into memory, for a woman whose heart was breaking.

"Don't weep, child," Charlotte whispered. "It's going to be all right. Compose yourself. David must not awaken to tears."

Hastily Sarah dabbed her eyes, grateful that the housekeeper should choose that moment at which to enter the room.

"Excuse me, ma'am."

Placing a tray on the bedside table she stood waiting, her hands clasped.

"What is it?" Charlotte demanded.

"There is a caller, ma'am. A gentleman."

"But didn't you tell him we are not receiving until after the funeral?" Charlotte fretted.

"I did, but he insisted."

"Then you shall see him, Sarah," Charlotte shrugged. "Explain that I will receive him later. Ask him to leave his card."

Smoothing her hair, straightening the folds of her skirt, Sarah sped down the stairs, glad to be away from the sickroom, to have cause to forget, if only for a few moments, the decision she had made.

The front door was open and a man stood on the topmost step. He was tall as a tree, his dark hair curling about his ears and the arrogant set of his head was endearingly, heartbreakingly familiar. Through the jumble of her thoughts and the mad, glad beating of her heart, Sarah heard herself say:

"Good-evening, Mr Midwinter."

"Good-evening, ma'am." Robey inclined his head gravely. "Can we talk — privately?"

"Please come in." Her voice was little more than a whisper.

"No. I'll not do that."

"Then a turn in the garden, perhaps?"

Oh, why were her legs so weak? Why was it so hard to breathe? She had made up her mind and there would be no going back, but did the sight of him have to torment her so? Did his nearness have to set her fingers tingling to touch him?

"They've let you go, Robey?" They'd had to, of course. The evidence they'd arrested him on was far too flimsy. Now, she thought with a shiver of relief, nothing need be told. No blame would attach itself to her father's name; no one need ever know that she and Robey had been lovers.

"Someone came forward," he nodded. "And

don't worry. They know nothing."

"Then how?"

She clenched her hands tightly for fear she should fling herself into his arms, willing him not to touch her lest her resolve should shatter.

"I'm leaving," he ground, ignoring her question. "Tomorrow. I came to tell you and say goodbye."

"Leaving?"

"Aye, and taking Maggie with me."

Near breathless, Sarah stopped in her tracks. Had he struck her, the pain could not have been more fierce. "But when I saw you there, I thought —"

"You thought I'd come for you, like I said. But things have changed. I'll have to take Maggie away from Hollinsdyke."

"But *why?*"

"Because I owe it to her," he insisted doggedly. "This morning she perjured herself for me. She told them at the police-station that she'd been with me on Moor Top hill. They didn't believe her, at first, so she told them we'd been making love there. When a woman as straight as Maggie Ormerod admits to something like that, they've no choice but to believe her. And I suppose," he shrugged, "they remembered what you'd said when they arrested me, about someone knowing where I was . . ."

"And now you think you owe her something?"

"I know I do, Sarah. What she told them isn't a thing to be admitted lightly. Maggie's a respectable girl and she'll lose her good name when it all gets around. Even in the Three-streets a woman doesn't give herself cheaply."

"I did, Robey."

"So you did, Mrs Holroyd," he acknowledged, as if her giving had counted for nothing. "Oh, and Maggie said to ask you to have a care for her folks. Her father's sick and there'll be no money coming in now."

His eyes met Sarah's calmly, his gaze steady. "She said you'd understand."

"Yes. Tell her not to worry," Sarah whispered, her lips so stiff it hurt her to speak. "I'll see they're well looked after."

He held out his hand, but she would not take it. To touch him would have been more than she could bear.

For a moment he looked into her eyes and she willed him with all the longing in her anguished heart to break down her resistance and take her in his arms just once more. But he did not touch her.

"Don't fret, Sarah," he said gently. "The police will let it drop now. There'll be no satisfaction gained by laying the blame on a dead man."

He smiled briefly, then with a toss of his head strode quickly away across the grass. At the belt of trees he stopped abruptly and, turning to face her, raising his hand in a farewell salute, he called softly:

"Goodbye, bonny lass."

"No!" Sarah cried. "No!" but he was gone,

disappearing from her sight in the blinking of an eye, and in the stillness around her it was as if he had never stood there, never spoken her name or looked at her with pity.

"God!" she moaned, hugging herself tightly, trying to stop the violent trembling of her body. She hadn't known how she would tell him, how she would find the strength to send him out of her life, yet he had given her no choice.

Maggie had lost her good name, but what had Sarah Holroyd lost? Now she would live with the knowledge that every time she looked at David, if God saw fit to spare him, she would remember what she had become.

Maggie had won. Gentle Maggie with the soft voice and tender blue eyes. Maggie had known she could never have Robey's love so she had made sure of the next best thing — his respect.

Sarah closed her eyes. The grass beneath her was tilting and her legs refused any longer to support her. Grief tearing at her heart she sank to her knees.

Lord, but it was almost *funny!* She had loved Robey so, been torn apart by the longing to follow him, yet he had never cared for her, not really cared. Not once, even in the spellbinding wonder of their loving, had he whispered the words she longed to hear.

Tears filled her eyes and she rocked back and forward on her knees, giving way to the tearing sobs that shook her body, cries born of despair and the searing pain of rejection. She had given all and there was nothing left, not even her self-respect. She, Sarah, was the loser.

And so Cook found her.

"Mrs David, ma'am," she puffed. "Oh, get up, do! Don't take on so. It's all right. He's going to get well!"

Clucking gently, she pulled Sarah to her feet, smiling into the tear-ravaged face.

"Don't grieve, ma'am. Mr David's awake. He's asking for you!"

A breeze lifted the lace curtains and the sun was warm on their faces as Sarah and David sat beside the open window of the bedroom.

It was impossible, she thought, looking out at the April garden and the hills of Moor Top green beyond it, to believe she could have lived through such torment.

The relief she felt at her husband's recovery had been overshadowed by the joyless duty of the burial of their dead.

Luke had been borne with great array to the iron-railed plot where all future Holroyds would lie, and Caleb her father had been laid to his rest beside the tiny, posy-strewn grave of the little orphan. She had found comfort in that. It seemed right they should be together.

"Goodbye, Father," she had whispered. "Take care of Billy-Boy for me. He's so little, so helpless . . ."

And now they were faced with a period of

mourning when their dress would be sombre and decorum demanded they should withdraw from social life for many months. The duty letters had been written on black-edged notepaper, the Charity Ball and all other engagements cancelled, and until society was satisfied that their dead had been sufficiently lamented they had to remain in self-imposed seclusion.

It suited Sarah very well. Such melancholy matched her mood. Now she was truly Sarah Holroyd, for all the trappings of her past were gone; her father, Billy-Boy, Maggie, Robey and the mill.

She had returned alone to Low Clough, standing among the ruins, gazing at the hollow windows that stared back at her like dead, accusing eyes. Only the counting-house remained and almost two hundred mill-workers from around the Three-streets had been made destitute.

David reached for Sarah's hand. He was paler, and thinner, but well at last and impatient to end his enforced convalescence.

"What are you thinking about?" he whispered. "There is such sadness in your eyes, Sarah. Can't you tell me?"

But it was a sadness that could not be shared. Guilt such as hers could not be absolved, or even halved by the telling. She had to bear it alone.

"I was thinking about the mill," she murmured. "What will you do about it?"

"We will rebuild, of course!"

"But is there the money?"

"Enough and to spare. My father was a cautious man and believed firmly in insurance. There'll be another Low Clough and, the sooner I can be up and about, the sooner we can make a start."

"Your mother is determined to leave," Sarah whispered. "I wish she would stay. There is so much I don't know about being a mill-master's wife. You'll have to be patient, David."

"There is all the time in the world. You'll soon get used to it."

All the time in the world, her heart echoed bleakly. A lifetime in which to learn, and to pay.

Outside, a lark soared singing into the sky, unhindered as the wind, and she followed it until her eyes were dazzled by the sunlight and its song could no longer be heard.

Sadly, David watched her. It was as if she had built her grief around her like an invisible shell and defied anyone to breach it. It was as though she had withdrawn into herself, determined to share her misery with no one. Her face was pale, her eyes large and luminous. He wanted to take her in his arms, shield her from the world, but he could not. She was a stranger.

"Why are you looking at me so?" Sarah demanded, a small smile playing briefly on her lips. "Is there a smut on my nose?"

"Your nose is perfect," he replied with forced gaiety. "Cannot a man look at his wife, especially when she is as lovely as you?"

"Please don't," she whispered. "You are so

kind, so warm-hearted, and I don't deserve you."

"Let me be the judge of that," he returned, taking her hands in his own.

"But how can you love me, David? You know so little about me."

"I know all I need to know," he smiled gently. "When I thought you were in danger, when the mill wall fell, it was as if my whole future flashed in front of my eyes and I saw it stretching empty, if you were not to be there to share it with me. And as for people saying I was brave — it wasn't any act of heroism made me fling you to safety. It was pure selfishness, because I was not prepared to live without you."

She stared at him mutely and he looked into her eyes, stark with torment, loving her so much that it throbbed aching inside him.

"Don't grieve," he pleaded. "You have suffered so much, but all sorrow passes. Nothing that is hurtful ever lasts. Believe me, Sarah."

All sorrow passes. Would that she could be sure of that. If only she could know that the guilt would diminish and the agony fade, if she could forget the hurt of a lover's betrayal, try harder to remember the bargain she had made with God.

Give him back and I will stay with him, try to love him as he loves me . . .

The lark was descending and she could hear its song once more. It had flown high into the sun and now it had to come down to earth again.

Once, Sarah yearned, she had briefly touched the stars and now she too had to free herself of all soaring memory and take her place at her husband's side. There was work to be done, promises to be kept. The sorrow would pass; David had promised it would.

"Oh, but we must build a fine new mill," she whispered fiercely. "It must be light and airy, a good place to work in. We must care for the orphans and those who are sick now because of Low Clough. Let's give it another name, so we can forget."

"No, the name shall remain," David insisted gently, "so we can *remember*."

She looked at him, longing to lay bare her soul, knowing she could not, had not to. There was only one way to receive absolution. She had to earn it.

"You will be well soon," she smiled. "When the doctor allows it, what shall we do?"

"We will get out of this room, out of this house," he laughed. "We will go to Moor Top hill. We shall walk and walk . . ."

She nodded, knowing how right he was. For him, it would be a happy return to where it had all begun; for her, there would be a ghost to lay, memories to banish and a promise to be renewed.

"Yes, David, we will walk the hills again," she whispered.

He looked at her with tenderness. There was pain in her eyes, still, and secrets he could never share. He knew it only too well, but suddenly the way ahead seemed clearer and in that instant he knew beyond all doubt that she would come to care for him as he cared for her. She would love him, given time, and until then his heart held love enough for the two of them.

Taking her hand he raised it to his lips and gently kissed the upturned palm.

"I love you, my Sarah," he whispered. "I shall love you always."

Always. It was a long time. It stretched into forever, but time was his. And he would wait.